Demon Hunters 4: Premonition

Demon Hunters 4
Premonition

Avril Sabine

Cracked Acorn Productions
Australia

Demon Hunters 4: Premonition

Published by

Cracked Acorn Productions

PO Box 1365

Gympie, Queensland 4570

Australia

978-1-925131-63-5 (Kindle)

978-1-925617-40-5 (EPUB)

978-1-925131-64-2 (Print)

Genre: Young Adult Urban Fantasy/Horror

Copyright 2016 © Avril Sabine

Cover design by Caitlyn Petersen

*For my oldest son. Thanks for all the
chocolate cakes and chocolate chip biscuits
while I was writing this book. And for coming
up with Cricket.*

Emily Hunter has had the same dream every night for the past six months, one that made her quit being a demon hunter. It's a nightmare she wishes never to have again. When she finally dreams of something else, it doesn't help, only has her fearing for her sanity and her life. To survive, she needs to face all she's tried to avoid. If she fails it'll mean not only her life is over, but also the life of a boy from her dreams. She knows only too well that when demons are involved, nightmares can come true.

*

This story was written by an Australian author using Australian spelling.

Chapter One

Emily struggled to escape the dream. She knew it had to be one, it was the only time she saw her parents. Night after night she watched them walk down the same corridor. Watched them come ever closer to the closed door at the far end, the beam of light from her father's torch shining on the warped timber, a sword in his other hand.

Beside him her mother held her bow, an arrow aimed at the closed door that continued to come closer. She wanted to scream at them to run. Tell them not to open the door. She should have told them the first time. Should have rung them when she'd dragged herself from sleep that first night to stare at the glowing numbers of her alarm clock. Two forty-five a.m. Those numbers would be forever inscribed in her mind. As was the scene she saw each time the door swung open.

The dream vanished, replaced by a scruffy brown dog looking up at her. Emily stared down at him. This had never happened before. She was always forced to see the dream through to the end. To eventually wake with tears streaming down her cheeks, an ache in her chest and a hollow feeling she didn't know what to do with. She wasn't sure if she should be relieved or worried to see the dog.

She guessed it was an Australian Terrier cross, taller than a Terrier at around forty-five centimetres, but with the typical look of one including the slightly darker markings down his back and around his muzzle. She had no idea why he'd invaded her dream. He took a couple of steps towards her, whining when she continued to look at him. Catching a glimpse of a tag on his collar, she bent down to read the name. Before she could touch the dog, a large cricket appeared in its place, staring at her for a second before it jumped away. She wanted to wake up. Unlike her usual dream there were no demons and no blood. Only darkness and a bad feeling.

She peered into the darkness, but could see nothing. She dreaded following. Dreaded what she'd find, but couldn't fight the urge to step into the dark. She ran into a letterbox that loomed up out of the darkness, the area around her becoming a foggy grey.

Stepping back from the metal letterbox, that was on a lean, she ran her fingers over the raised numbers on the front. Seventy-eight. What did it mean? Or did it mean nothing? Looking past the letterbox, the dread she'd been feeling increased. She wanted to wake up. Knowing she was dreaming should make it easier to wake. It didn't. She had six months of nightmare filled nights to prove it. Even ordering herself to wake up didn't help. She was as trapped as her parents had been.

Stepping around the letterbox, she kept moving forward. The darkness receded with each step, the area around her full of murky shadows. Her right hand tightened into a fist and she wished she had her bow. It appeared in her hand and she stared down at it, reaching for an arrow out of the quiver that was now on her back. It didn't make her feel any better. Only waking would do that.

A house loomed out of the darkness ahead of her, no lights showing at the windows. Hearing a whining sound, she walked silently around to the back of the house. She stopped when she saw the dog stood on his back legs to scratch at a window ledge. She tried to fight it, but couldn't prevent herself from moving forward to peer in the window. Behind her she could hear the ticking of a clock, but when she glanced over her shoulder there was only darkness. She had a feeling time was running out. But she didn't know who for. Herself? The dog? Someone else? Not her parents, their time had already run out. Six months ago on a trip to Brisbane.

The window came closer. Would it be like the room when her father had opened the door? Was this only another angle of the same dream? If so, why the dog? Lowering the bow, she shut her eyes as she felt herself lean forward. The glass of the window was cold against her face, but she refused to look. Doubted she could cope with any more gory details. Falling asleep was difficult enough these days without adding anything else to keep her from it.

"Midway upon the journey of our life, I found myself within a forest dark, for the straightforward pathway had been lost."

The familiar words caused her to open her eyes and she stared into the room, trying to place the quote. Shock held her in place when she wanted to run. She dreaded to find out what would happen next. Her legs wouldn't obey and she met the gaze of a boy around her age, chained to a solid timber bed. He stretched out a hand to her, his brown eyes pleading with her to help. She shook her head. She couldn't help him. She hadn't been able to help her parents.

But she wanted to help him. Something about him had her feeling as if she knew him, or should know him. Closing her eyes she immediately opened them, unable to face the sight of the blood she regularly saw in the darkness of her mind. She'd been seeing it ever since that first nightmare. The one that had come true.

The boy was gone, flames leaping across the bed he'd been chained to. She dropped the arrow, her hand covering her mouth to hold in the scream that threatened to escape at the sight of the flames. She took a step back. Had he been burned alive? Turning, she ran, the dog appearing at her side, footsteps behind her. She didn't look. Didn't want to know what followed. A street sign came out of the darkness and she stumbled, trying to avoid it. Grabbing hold of the post, she looked up, the name seared into her mind along with the number she'd seen earlier. Beyond the sign she saw the moon, a narrow crescent in the sky.

"All hope abandon, ye who enter here."

Hearing the words spoken behind her, she spun to see the boy, realising what this and the earlier quote were from. "Dante."

He reached for her, wearing no shirt and blood smeared across his chest from shallow cuts. Before he could make contact she woke, gasping for breath, sitting up to swing her legs to the floor, nausea making her stomach churn.

She reached for the bedside lamp, her gaze scanning the room the moment it was filled with light. She was safe. Nothing was in the room. Yet she couldn't resist sliding her fingers between the mattress and the bed base. A touch of relief started to fill her when she felt the dagger. Withdrawing her hand, she absently rubbed at her demon mark. It was a narrow black line with a hint of red in it that started at the pulse point in the middle of her wrist and travelled to the outside, wrapping around once. It was part of her skin, not a tattoo as many people assumed, and was gained from dealing with demons. It burned or itched when demons were in the area, depending on the power of the demon, but now it was fine. The only demons were the ones in her nightmare. Ones that had plagued her every night.

Her gaze stopped on the alarm clock. Two forty-five a.m. Closing her eyes, she clutched the edge of the bed, trying to slow her breathing. It didn't help. She wanted to scream or throw up. Instead she opened her eyes, slowly rose to her feet and crossed the room. Reminding herself to remain calm, she rested her head on the bedroom door for a moment, grounding herself in reality. It had only been a dream. Images of her parents' funeral came to her. Some nightmares did come true. Pain arrowed through her and she swung the door open, her jaw clenched tight as she fought against it.

She forced all thoughts from her mind, trying to focus on her surroundings. The rest of the house was silent and she crept along the hallway. Her uncles were probably in bed. They weren't really her uncles. They were her grandfather's nephews. But when you had a large extended family like hers, it often became confusing keeping track of how everyone was related. It was easier to simplify things.

Reaching the guest bathroom, she turned on the light and made her way to the vanity. She gripped the edge of the sink for a moment before turning on the tap and splashing water on her face. It didn't help. She hadn't expected to dispel the feelings her dream had left her with that easily. But it had been worth a try. She stared at herself in the mirror, trying to figure out if the shadows under her hazel eyes were worse or if it was from the harsh bathroom light. She feared they were worse. But what could she expect when her sleep was continually broken by nightmares?

Pushing dark, honey coloured hair away from her face, she turned her back on the mirror. She couldn't keep this up. Couldn't continue to go night after night with very little sleep. Not that she had any idea what she could do to change things. Nothing she'd tried so far had worked.

Striding from the bathroom she headed outside, stopping on the verandah that went the perimeter of the house. The cool night air washed over her making it difficult to believe how hot it had been yesterday. Although she guessed she shouldn't complain. January in the northern outskirts of Brisbane was far cooler than where she lived in Mackay.

Hearing footsteps she spun, her body tensed to fight. Seeing it was Leo she tried to relax, but her heart continued to race and she remained alert, waiting for an attack that wasn't coming. "Did I wake you?" She'd tried to be quiet.

Leo shrugged. "I'm a light sleeper. Those brothers of mine keep me awake most of the night with their snoring. Was it Adam and Saul's snoring that woke you?" He was in his early forties, was both tall and broad and his beard had a touch of grey in amongst the brown. His head was shaved and creases radiated out from his blue eyes when he smiled.

She tried to return his smile, but wasn't sure how successful she was. Her gaze was drawn to the flannelette shirt he wore with faded denim jeans. She was tempted to ask him if he slept in a flannelette shirt as well as wearing one every day. She searched around for something to say. "I've nearly finished cataloguing another book for Gran." She'd arrived six days ago for her cousin Charlotte's wedding and had used helping to catalogue the family's extensive library on demons, as an excuse not to return home. She'd hoped the change of scenery would help with the nightmares. It looked like she was wrong. She was beginning to fear nothing would and she'd be tormented by them for years.

Leo tucked his hands into his pockets. "Uncle Tim and Aunt Cathy rang while you were taking a walk earlier. I didn't expect you to be gone so long. I told them I'd get you to ring when you returned. They rang a second time."

She'd been trying to avoid all of them. Or more accurately the looks they gave her. The ones that asked, without words, if she was okay. "Did Grandad and Grandma say what they wanted?"

"To see how you are. They miss you. I think they're wondering when you're going home. Or if you are."

She looked away from him, noticing the moon. It reminded her of the one in her dream. A crescent that was a little thinner than the one she'd dreamt of. A shiver went through her as she tried to stop images from the dream invading her mind. "Is that your way of saying I've overstayed my welcome?" She looked over her shoulder at him, her head tilted slightly to the side, away from her shoulder, as she tried to figure out his expression.

"You're welcome to stay as long as you like, Emily." The creases around his eyes disappeared and his voice was soft.

With a slight nod she returned her gaze to the moon. What had her dream meant? She didn't want to be like Gran. Didn't want to dream of the future. The only time she had, and she still wasn't completely certain if it had been a premonition, was when her parents had died. She'd had plenty of nightmares before and none of them had come true. Not a single one. She'd planned to ask Gran about her dream, after the wedding, but with everything that happened that day she hadn't been able to bring herself to speak to her about it.

"You do know we're here if you ever want to talk about anything. Anything at all."

Continuing to watch the moon, she nodded. She hadn't been able to tell anyone. She didn't know which would be worse. Fearing for her sanity or having premonitions. If it was the latter, then she'd let her parents die. She'd had the chance to save them, but had done nothing about it, thinking it had only been a bad dream. She didn't know if she could live with that.

"Did you want something to help you sleep? They always offer warm milk in the movies."

This time her smile came easily. She faced Leo. "Maybe in movies from your generation. In mine, they offer alcohol."

Chuckling, Leo shook his head. "That's not going to happen. Not until you're eighteen. Ask me again in October."

She hadn't expected him to agree. Yawning, she covered her mouth. "I might head back to bed." If she was lucky she'd manage to fall into a dreamless sleep.

"You let me know if you need anything." He clapped her on the back.

She staggered forward slightly, even though she'd been expecting it and had braced herself. "Okay." Leaving Leo on the verandah, she returned to her room. Again she yawned and, taking it as a positive sign, dropped onto the bed. Turning out the light she lay in the dark, waiting for sleep to arrive. It didn't.

It wasn't until the darkness of the room became grey that she fell asleep. She guessed it wasn't long after she'd fallen asleep that her usual dream started and she was forced to relive her parents' last night all over again. No matter how hard she tried, she couldn't wake. Guilt washed over her as she watched her parents come closer to the door and did nothing to stop them. Even in her dream she couldn't warn them. It wasn't until the multitude of demons in the room had slaughtered her parents, blood staining the walls and floor that she was able to wake.

Chapter Two

She sat up, swinging her legs to the floor, resting her elbows on her knees to clutch her head when it dropped forward. Her throat was tight with the need to cry, but she'd done far too much of that already. There had to be a way to stop dreaming. If there was, she couldn't think of it. Nothing had helped, not even exhaustion. Maybe she should ring Gran and ask her when she had the time to talk. She needed to figure out what was going on. Maybe she hadn't let her parents die after all. Maybe it had only been a coincidence.

The words rang falsely in her mind. Yeah, like she believed that. Instead of calling them the first time she'd been woken by the dream she'd stared at the numbers on her alarm clock, telling herself it was only a dream. None of her other dreams had ever come true. The dream had felt different and yet she'd still ignored it, going back to sleep while her parents were being torn apart by demons.

She rose abruptly, unable to think about it any longer. Not without curling up in a ball on her bed and spending the rest of the day staring at the wall, tears endlessly falling. She forced herself to get ready for the morning and make her way to the study she was using to work on the catalogue. Slipping on the dark framed glasses she wore for close vision work, she sat at the desk and continued reading the book, making notes as she went.

The book she was working on had a section about creatures that were as old as demons and often were mistaken for them. They'd also been worshipped as gods, a long time ago. These days they'd mostly retreated from the world. She didn't blame them. Retreating from the world sounded enticing, but she doubted it would stop the nightmares.

It took her far longer to finish the book than she'd expected, as she also had to figure out how to categorise the details from that section in the catalogue. She finally reached the end and closed the book, staring at the leather bound item, the title a worn indent across the front. Maybe this wasn't the best idea. Maybe reading about demons day after day was making it impossible for her to stop having that dream. Leaving the book on the desk and removing her glasses, she rose to her feet and stretched. Her stomach growled in protest over how long it had been since she'd eaten.

The kitchen was empty and, relieved, she made herself some food before heading outside for a walk. She didn't think she could talk to anyone. For some reason she was finding it harder than usual to push the dreams away. Both the dreams. Thinking about her nights, she ended up walking much further than she'd planned and had to hurry to get back before dark. Reaching the house as the light faded from the sky, she searched for her three uncles, thinking she should probably let them know she was back. They were sure to have noticed her absence by now. She found Leo in the lounge room, watching the news on the television. She stared at the image on the screen. A buzzing sound filled her ears and she clutched the door frame to keep her legs from giving way, her heart racing fast enough she feared it might burst from her chest.

The boy from her dream was on the screen. He grinned at her, brown eyes with a hint of mischief, short black hair and his arm around a dog that sat on a tree stump cut off at waist height. The same dog she'd seen in her dream. The photo of him was replaced by a weeping woman, a boy and a girl on either side of her. A reporter asked her a question, but all she could do was burst into tears. The teenage boy stepped protectively in front of the woman to glare at the reporter. He looked similar to the boy from her dream. Similar enough that he was probably his brother. The girl had dark brown hair like her mother, but the same eyes as the missing boy. Although hers were lacking the hint of mischief, filled instead with tears.

An ad came on as the buzzing sound stopped and Emily realised she was trembling. She continued to hold onto the door frame, since her legs still felt like they were about to give way and dump her on the floor. She stared at the woman on the ad, her smile wide, teeth perfect, blue eyes shining, blond hair falling in waves around her shoulders and her skin flawless. The ideal model to advertise Eternally Flawless Beauty Cream, a jar of which momentarily replaced the woman on the screen. The insignificance of the ad, compared to seeing the boy from her dream, made the moment seem more surreal. She had to get out of here before she lost it.

"I'm going for a drive." She was surprised at how steady her voice sounded. Surprised she was still standing.

Leo turned to face her. "What about dinner?"

Somehow she managed to shrug and let go of the door frame without collapsing on the floor. "I'll grab something while I'm out." Turning, she forced herself to walk slowly away when all she wanted to do was run. In her bedroom, she collected the satchel she used instead of a handbag and her car keys. Her phone was already in the satchel. She had no idea how she was still standing. It felt like she was an observer of a distant world. How was she ever going to survive knowing she'd let her parents die? Pain arrowed through her and she clenched her jaw as she fought against being overwhelmed by it.

On the front verandah she pulled on her boots, grabbing the wall of the low set house when she nearly fell over. It was probably a bad idea to be driving right now, but she needed to get out of the house. Needed to be by herself while she tried to figure everything out. Her thoughts were a confusing mess. She alternated between believing she had premonitions and was responsible for the death of her parents, that the world was full of crazy coincidences or she was hallucinating and seeing things that hadn't really happened. She didn't know which option was worse.

She didn't make it all the way to the highway

before she had to pull over and turn off the engine of her four-wheel-drive, sitting in the dark. Resting her head against the steering wheel, she tried to stop shaking. What was going on? She'd never seen the boy before in her life. Why had she dreamt of him? Or maybe she had seen him. Maybe she'd caught a glimpse of a news report and not taken it in properly. She nearly groaned at how desperate she was for it to be anything other than having premonitions. There was nothing special about her. No reason why she should have such dreams when in four generations there'd been no one other than Gran who'd had them. It wasn't possible.

Raising her head, she turned on the interior light and took her phone from the satchel and opened up a web browser, keying in the street name from her dream. She pulled up the street image and checked the houses one by one. Her breath caught in her throat. That was it. That was the house from her dream. It wasn't possible. She slowly shook her head. It couldn't be. Maybe she was mistaken. She continued to stare at the screen of the phone until it went black, her heart pounding loudly in the silence, her breath coming in jagged gasps that sounded far too much like sobs.

There was only one way to find out if any of it

was real. It took her longer than she'd expected to calm herself enough to drive. After fighting demons for so many years, she hadn't expected to be falling apart like this. Not over a photo on the news. But she guessed nothing she'd experienced had prepared her for this. It was a good thing she'd quit being a hunter when her parents had died. She'd been right to fear her ability to cope. Demon hunters always fought in pairs, sometimes groups. The last thing she'd wanted to do was get more of her family killed.

As soon as her hands were reasonably steady she put the address into the GPS, turned off the interior light and started the vehicle. When she pulled out onto the highway she was glad the traffic was unusually light for a Saturday night. She doubted she could have coped in heavy traffic. Not with the way her head was reeling.

She glanced towards the GPS, trying to control the fear that raced through her. She was a demon hunter. Well, she had been until she'd quit six months ago. Now she didn't know what she was. Or what to do with her life. She'd always expected to be a hunter. Protecting humans from the world they didn't know existed. Facing creatures most people thought only belonged in movies, games and books. She had to remain calm, had to remember her training. Falling apart wasn't an option. She'd already done that and it hadn't helped.

Turning onto the street, she pulled up and forced herself to get out of the vehicle. She stared at the sign lit by the nearby streetlight. It was exactly the same as the one in her dream. Dragging her gaze from the sign she looked further along the street. If the sign was real, how much more of her dream was? Hopefully not the dog turning into a cricket. Although that was always possible if demons were involved.

A movement to her left had her heart racing and she nearly laughed at herself when a dog crept out of the shadows created by a flowering shrub. The urge to laugh faded when the dog took several more steps towards her into a pool of light cast by the streetlight. Her legs refused to support her and she ended up on the grass of the footpath, the scruffy brown dog pressing his wet nose against her cheek.

She tried to take several deep breaths, but couldn't slow down her breathing. This wasn't happening. Maybe it was yet another nightmare she couldn't escape from. The dog pressed his wet nose against her cheek again, whining. She'd felt hot and cold in her dreams, but never liquid. Even blood didn't feel real in her nightmares no matter how realistic it appeared.

The light reflected off a tag at the dog's neck and she stared at it. "You better not turn into a cricket." The dog wagged his narrow tail, looking far too happy about her warning. "I'm serious." It took her nearly a minute to reach for the tag and read what was engraved on it. She was glad she was already sitting. "Cricket." Letting go of the tag she closed her eyes and tightened her hand into a fist to try and stop the shaking. It didn't help. The dream rushed in on her. How much of it had been real and how much a metaphor?

The words from 'Dante's Inferno' came to mind. 'All hope abandon, ye who enter here.' She really hoped they were metaphorical. When Cricket whined, she opened her eyes to stare at him. "You want to show me where he is, don't you?" Cricket whined again.

She struggled to her feet, wondering if she should call someone. She pushed that thought aside. She was a trained hunter. Her family name was Hunter. Even her father had taken on her mother's name when they'd married, also becoming a hunter. She could do this. It was past time she stopped hiding away. It wouldn't change the past, but maybe it would help if she changed the future of the boy she'd seen chained up in her dream. If only she'd known six months ago that her dreams had become more than common nightmares.

Striding to the back of her vehicle, even though her legs wanted to give out on her, she opened it up and stared at the backpack that always remained in there. When she'd quit she hadn't been able to take it out. It had seemed so final, like losing her parents all over again. She reached for it, trying to ignore the tremble in her hand. She hadn't felt this afraid since the first time she'd faced a demon when she was fourteen. She'd done this numerous times before. Well, not rescued someone, but fought demons. And she guessed that was what all this was about. Nothing else made sense. Or as much sense as things could make when demons were involved.

She rummaged in the backpack and took out two small vials of holy water, a box of matches, a small torch and the small case of lock picks her father had taught her how to use years ago. He'd taught her a lot of different skills over the years. Ones most demon hunters wouldn't have approved of. Her mother hadn't. When she'd tried to ask her father about his life before he'd met her mother, all he'd say was it had been different. She suspected that had been an understatement.

She hesitated over the metal box that ran across

the back of the vehicle, pressed against the back seat. It was locked with a combination padlock. The dog whining beside her helped make up her mind. It had been in the dream. There was a good chance she'd need it. And if those words from 'Dante's Inferno' were more than metaphorical she would definitely need it. She dialled in the numbers. 300666. The hour of demons and the devil's number. A lot of Hunters used it so that in an emergency other Hunters would have access to weapons.

Opening the lid of the box she withdrew her bow and quiver of arrows, leaving the spare bundles of arrows in the box. There were a dozen in the quiver. If she needed more than that she'd be in serious trouble. She couldn't prevent thoughts of the blood filled room, her parents had been found in, coming to mind. She'd only ever seen it in her dreams, but that was more than enough.

Locking up the vehicle, she put the keys in the little box fixed beneath it for that purpose. Straightening, her hand tightened around the bow, she stared down the street. She was ready. Or as ready as she was likely to be. She tried to ignore the fear, but no matter how often she told herself she could do this, it remained. Looking down at the dog, she watched him for a moment before she spoke. "Okay, Cricket. Where to?"

The dog looked up at her, wagging his tail.

She sighed. He'd been much more helpful in her dream. Apart from how he'd turned into a cricket and left her behind. Looking down the street again, she forced herself to head towards the first house. A glance at it showed her it was nothing like the one in her dream. She kept going.

Cricket ran ahead of her, becoming lost in the long stretch of shadows created by a streetlight with a broken bulb.

Stopping, she stared after him. She had a bad feeling that was her destination. It took far longer than it should for her to start moving again. She passed two houses, freezing when she reached the third. Her gaze was fixed on the letterbox. It was metal, on a lean and had the number seventy-eight on the front. Like she'd done in the dream, she couldn't resist running her fingers over the raised numbers. Some of the edges were rough, a detail that hadn't been in her dream. It might feel like a nightmare, but she was definitely in the real world. Her gaze slowly rose and she stared at the house set well back from the footpath.

Chapter Three

Emily's legs felt like they might give way again and she clutched the letterbox. When it made a groaning sound she let go, fearing it might break. Cricket came running out of the shadows from beside the house. She pressed a hand to her mouth, holding back the scream she'd nearly let escape before she'd realised what the movement was.

She stared at the dog that stopped at her feet, tail wagging. She couldn't see his expression, but she wouldn't have been surprised if it was something along the lines of 'what's taking you so long'. She was tempted to tell him, then had to bite back a nervous laugh when she reminded herself he was a dog. "Okay, boy. Lead the way." When he did she followed him to the side of the house, taking out her torch and turning it on. A pool of light shining on the ground didn't make her feel any better. If anything, it reminded her of the dream. She shined the light ahead, trying to see Cricket. He was nowhere in sight. He'd raced off without her again. Her grip tightened on the torch.

Heading for the back of the house, she found herself jumping at every sound. No matter how many times she kept telling herself she was a well-trained hunter, she couldn't stop thinking about her parents. They'd had far more experience than her. Reaching the corner of the house, she peered around it. Cricket stood on his hind legs scratching at the ledge of a window, partway along the building. With the mild itch she was feeling in her demon mark there was definitely a demon in the area. Either he was minor or not close enough to make the mark burn. She should return to the vehicle and use the phone she'd left in her satchel. Gran would know what to do. After all, Brisbane was her neighbourhood. She started to turn away then decided she'd have a look in the window so she could let Gran know exactly what the problem was.

Each step she took sounded loud and she wished Cricket would stop scratching the timber window ledge. The noise was far louder than she liked. Reaching his side, she tucked the torch under the arm she carried the bow with and tugged on his collar.

"Sit." The dog obeyed immediately. Taking hold of the torch, she shined it in the window. It was hard to see what was in the room with her reflection peering back at her.

She pressed her face and the torch against the glass, the cold reminding her of her dream. Moving the beam of light across the room she froze, swamped by the memory of her dream, trying to figure out what was real and what wasn't. He was lying on a bed on the far side of the room, one hand stretched out and chained to the timber bed head. His back was to her and he was wearing only jeans. There were dark stains on his skin, what looked like smeared, bloody handprints. His hair was short and a dark colour, and his body was fit, the muscles clearly defined. It wouldn't have helped. You needed more than physical strength when facing demons.

The boy rolled over and stared at her, his dark eyes pleading, his free hand reaching for her as he sat up.

She felt the demon before she heard him, the itch in her demon mark becoming a slight burn. She spun to face him, listening to Cricket run away with a whimper. She didn't blame him. She wanted to run too. The heat of the demon rolled over her, the smell of him like the metallic scent of blood, a smoky bonfire and a touch of sulphur blended together. He was about six and a half feet tall and looked human. Looking like a bouncer at a nightclub, wearing a black t-shirt and jeans, his arms were crossed against his chest and his stance wide. The world seemed to shift and change and the fear and uncertainty she'd felt for the past six months gave way as the years of training kicked in.

She looked him up and down, wondering what he really looked like when he wasn't trying to appear human. "Show me your true face, demon." Behind her the boy called out for help.

"Don't try and order me around, hunter." The demon glanced at her wrist. "I know what you are and I don't fear any of you. Shall I tell you how many hunters I've killed over the centuries? Starting with the most recent?"

She didn't want to know which hunters he'd killed. Not right now. If he was one of the demons who'd been in the house she saw in her nightmares she didn't know what she might do. Maybe she'd be better off if she didn't see his face. Her hand tightened on her bow and torch as she forced down a second demand for him to show her his true face. She needed to focus on what was happening now, not remember the past. "What are you called?"

He laughed. "You think to use my name against me?"

She shook her head. Why hadn't she called Gran? Why had she thought she'd needed more information before ringing? "No. I want to know the name of the demon I will return to hell." She couldn't decide if she should drop the torch and grab an arrow or slowly move towards the side of the house, where there was more light, before she attacked. She heard the boy call out again, begging for help. She hated having to ignore him.

The demon laughed once more. "You're very amusing for a human. As well as terribly helpful turning up here like this. It'll save me going hunting. You humans seem to be finally learning wariness. It took you long enough."

"What name are you going by?"

"Flawless."

His words filled her with an unwanted certainty. But she had to ask. "Eternally Flawless?" His grin was the only answer she needed. Dropping the torch, she reached for an arrow, firing it at the demon as she dodged to the side. She felt the rush of air as he attacked. Spinning away, she ran for the side of the house, needing light to be able to accurately aim at him. Feeling the heat of Flawless rushing in on her, she stopped and faced him as she drew another arrow and fitted it to the bow.

The demon roared when the arrow pierced his body. "You will die painfully, hunter."

She didn't bother to answer, running around the side of the house, another arrow in her hand. Most hunters died a painful death. Demons never showed them any mercy. Halfway along the side of the house she stopped, staring at the woman who stepped around the corner. The woman pointed a gun at her and was the same smiling woman from the ad she'd seen earlier. There was no way she could escape. This was why hunters fought in pairs. She aimed the arrow at the woman. Behind her she felt the demon. She fired, moving to the side in the hope the demon wouldn't get her. Drawing another arrow she tried to focus on her options instead of fearing she'd die here alone. There didn't seem to be many.

It took her a second to realise that instead of attacking, the demon had rushed past her to take the arrow that had been meant for the woman. He ripped the arrow from his flesh, roaring as liquid darkened the shoulder of his shirt and ran down his arm in dark rivulets.

She thought of her maternal grandparents. They had no other children than her mother and she had no siblings. She didn't know if they'd survive her death, they'd barely survived the death of their daughter. Her paternal grandparents had other sons and grandchildren, but they would struggle too. Drawing another arrow, she aimed it at the demon. "I will be missed."

It was the woman who answered. "It doesn't matter. We're preparing to leave this area anyway. It never pays to stay in one location for long."

Before she could reply, Emily was tackled from behind by a demon. She hadn't noticed him until he was right on her. It was easy to miss so minor a demon when there was a major one around. She wanted to struggle, but remained still. She couldn't match a demon's strength, but maybe she could out think him.

The woman turned to Flawless. "Put her in with the boy. I'll be back before three to supervise." She glanced around. "And make sure none of the neighbours saw anything. If they did, deal with them."

The demon continued to pin Emily to the ground and she kept hold of her bow. She needed information if she had any hope of surviving the night. "Why would you do this? Why get mixed up with demons? You could lose everything, including your business."

The woman looked back over her shoulder, having been about to leave. "You have no idea, do you?" The woman turned to Flawless. "I thought you said these hunters were meant to be smart. Something to be feared. None of them we've encountered so far have been anything worth worrying about."

"It's the old ones you have to watch. They're the canny ones."

Emily could no longer stop the words that burst from her. "What other hunters are you talking about?"

The woman didn't bother answering, striding away.

Emily looked at Flawless. "What hunters?" She was related to all the hunters in Brisbane. Actually, she was probably related to nearly every demon hunter in Australia and some of the ones overseas if you counted all of her extremely extended family.

Flawless looked past her to the demon holding her down. "Essence, you heard Susan. Lock her up with the boy."

"You do not order me around." There was an edge to Essence's voice.

Flawless grinned mockingly. "I order around any who are less powerful than me."

Emily watched as Flawless headed in the same direction Susan had taken. The moment Essence released his grip on her, she rolled away, getting to her feet. She automatically drew an arrow and aimed it at the demon, who didn't look in the least bit human.

He grinned at her, sharp cat like teeth matching the pointed ears on his slightly feline head. He had bat wings and his feet and hands ended in long claws. His leathery skin was a dark charcoal, a slightly darker colour making a snake like pattern across his skin. "I can steal life from you while you live with only my touch. Drop the bow and arrow and I'll wait until you're dead." He cackled, a sound that would have went perfectly with a cartoon character witch. "I much prefer to do it when you're alive. The pain you'll feel is entertaining."

She wanted to argue with him, wanted to ask him what was going on. Instead, she slowly reduced the tension on the string and dropped first the arrow and then her bow. When he gestured towards her quiver, she removed it as well. A life stealing demon was too dangerous to mess with, no matter how minor he currently was. She glanced towards the road.

Running wasn't an option. She wouldn't reach her vehicle before the demon could catch her.

"Around the back." He gestured in the direction he wanted her to take.

With one last look at her weapon and ammunition, she turned and headed towards the back of the house. At least she still had her holy water. She scanned the area, trying to find some way of escaping. There was nothing. At the back she caught a glimpse of Cricket, wishing she could send him for help.

"Move faster. There's a door at the end of the house."

She couldn't help glancing at the window as she walked past. It was too dark to see inside and the boy was once again silent. Coming to the door, she reached out to open it, freezing. She was shocked to see her hand wasn't shaking. Not even slightly. How many times had she stared at shaking hands after a nightmare? She'd lost count. It felt like a piece of a puzzle falling into place. This she understood. This she'd been trained for and lived with her entire life. Dreaming about her parents' death before it occurred, that she didn't understand. Maybe she hadn't needed to quit hunting for fear she'd get a partner killed.

"Move, hunter."

There was no time to finish figuring it out.

Opening the door, she glanced around once more. It looked like she'd have to wait until the demon left her before she tried to escape. She stepped into a laundry. The demon brushed past her to lead the way.

Chapter Four

The demon eventually stopped in a hallway in front of a room and looked Emily up and down. "Have you any weapons?"

"You're not going to search me?"

He cackled. "What need have I for your useless human methods when I can hear the truth and lies in your words?"

She'd suspected as much when he'd asked instead of searching her, but it was good to have it confirmed. There were ways to lie while still telling the truth. "I have holy water."

"Put it on the floor." He pointed to a spot against the wall.

It didn't surprise her that he was reluctant to touch it. Holy water burned demons. Which is why she dipped her arrows in it. Flawless was going to feel the pain from her arrows for hours. Maybe days if she was lucky. She felt grim satisfaction as she placed one of the vials on the floor.

"Is someone out there?"

She looked towards the door, wondering if she should answer the boy who'd called out.

"Anyone?"

"Shut up." Essence glared at the door for a moment before returning his gaze to Emily. "Have you a phone?"

She shook her head. "Not on me. I left it behind."

"Any other ways of calling for help?"

"You mean other than screaming?"

"Don't be smart, hunter. Answer the question."

"No."

"Any other weapons?"

She vaguely gestured to where her bow had been left. "You made me leave my bow and arrows outside."

"No knives?"

She shook her head. "Do I look like the sort of person capable of taking a demon on at close range? I have no knives on me." She sometimes did, but that wasn't the question he'd asked.

He stared at her a moment longer before he looked towards the door. There was a click and it swung open. "Inside." He nodded towards the door.

She was surprised at how much effort it took to step inside the dark room. It looked nothing like the one her parents had entered, but it made her think of it. Maybe it was the thought of entering a trap. Trying to see the room clearly, she wished she had her torch. The only light in there was what filtered through from the hallway and window. The boy stood beside the bed, a dark shadow in the corner of the room.

"Move it."

She turned to face the demon. He was far closer than she preferred. She took a step back from him. "Where to? You only said to go inside."

"What's going on?" the boy demanded.

Essence ignored him. "Near the boy, human."

She did as he ordered, thinking of her dream. Maybe she'd needed to be captured to be able to help him escape. She hoped so. She dreaded to think what would happen if they couldn't get away before three a.m. Once the demon left, she could use the lock picks on the padlock attached to the chain wrapped around the boy's wrist. Stopping beside him she could see cuts on his chest and blood smeared across his skin. She was pretty sure they were handprints or at least hand like prints. She blinked several times when the demon turned the light switch on before coming towards them.

"Why won't anyone tell me what's going on?"

"If you don't shut up, you will regret it." The demon's gaze was drawn to the boy's chest. "And I will enjoy it."

Emily elbowed the boy when he tried to speak again. When he started to speak once more, she glared at him. "Quiet." She was tempted to ask if he was an idiot. Not that she was any better. She shouldn't have come here alone. That had been crazy.

The demon cackled. "You should listen to the hunter, human." The demon stared at the boy, not speaking until he'd remained quiet for a moment. "Hold out your hand." The demon growled when the boy held out his free hand. "The other one."

The chain rattled when he held it out. Essence grabbed hold of him and the boy tried to pull away. There was a snap and the padlock opened. The moment the chain was off his wrist, the boy tried to escape.

Essence slammed him against the wall, the impact loud in the silent room. "I warned you." He drew back his hand, claws aimed at the boy's chest.

Fear for the boy race through Emily and she grabbed Essence's wrist, her hand wrapping around his leathery skin. "No. Wait. He doesn't understand how powerful demons can be."

Essence kept his hand still even though he could have easily broken away from her grip. "You know how powerful I am?"

She had to be careful with what she said since this demon could hear the lies in her words. She knew he wasn't powerful. Nowhere near as powerful as Flawless. Essence was the kind of demon who would be able to walk about in the daylight, not bothered by it. Flawless wouldn't be able to. "I've spent my life learning about demons."

Essence released the boy, but allowed Emily to keep hold of his wrist. "Can you tell how powerful I am, hunter?"

She held the demon's gaze. No demon liked to be thought lacking in power. "Of course I can, demon. But what matter is the power you have now when you are constantly adding to it?" She tried to remain calm, tried to ignore the fear being this close to a demon caused. The evening had been full of stupid choices.

Essence cackled, drawing his arm from her grip. "Very good, hunter. And when the hour of three arrives, your power will add to mine." He gestured to the boy who remained against the wall, listening to their conversation. "His essence will give others extended life."

When the boy made a break for it, Emily got in his way before the demon could. She pressed against his shoulders, trying to force him back against the wall. "Make it easy on yourself. You can't escape now." She met his brown eyes, fear and confusion filling them. She knew those emotions intimately. "Don't enter a fight you can't win." She fought against the pain that washed over her at having used her father's words. Why hadn't he followed his own advice?

"Hold out your hands. Both of you."

When the boy didn't move, she whispered, "Please." Taking his hand, she held out both of hers, her hand grasping hold of his.

The demon wrapped the chain around their hands that were clasped together, hooking the padlock through so the chain was tight against them. He clicked it shut, letting go with a grin, his sharp teeth gleaming in the overhead light. "I will see you before the hour of three." He reached for Emily, who'd lowered her arms, still holding the boy's hand. "What were you wanting for your cooperation?"

His claws grasped hold of her chin and she remained still, not wanting to risk him breaking the skin. There was no way she wanted any demon to have her blood. "I will think on it."

"I thought you must already have something in mind."

"I have several things in mind, but I know how important it is to word things correctly around demons."

Essence cackled, releasing her. "Your words ring with truth, hunter." He turned away, without even a glance for the boy, and strode to the door. Turning the light off, he left.

The sound of a click when the door was locked behind him sounded so final and Emily forced herself to remain still as her initial urge to run faded. A glance around the room showed mostly shadows, with scant light coming in the window.

"What-"

She covered his mouth with her free hand. "Shh."

He turned his head away. "Don't."

She pushed him against the wall. Did he want to get them killed? "Quiet." She tried to hear if there was anyone nearby. There was only silence. Not that it meant much. Stepping back, she sighed. "Sorry."

"Can I talk now?"

"Yeah. Quietly though." She drew the matches from her pocket, letting go of his hand to try and turn hers in the chains. It was difficult, but she eventually managed it.

"Who are you and what are you doing? Why did that thing keep calling you hunter?"

Maybe she should have told him he couldn't talk. She lit a match, scanning the room. She really should have done that earlier. She'd been trained better than that. "Emily Hunter." Shaking the match out before it burned her fingers, she dropped it onto the floor and lit another one. She had no idea what time it was, but she wanted to be gone well before three a.m.

"What?"

She couldn't help smiling at his look of confusion. "My name. It's Emily Hunter. What's yours?"

"Dan Mills."

She frowned at him before she shook the match out, the lines from her dream coming to her. "Midway upon the journey of our life I found myself within a forest dark, for the straightforward pathway had been lost." She lit another match, having no idea what had made her say the quote aloud.

"How did you know?"

She had no idea what he was talking about, but as she watched him, his confusion cleared.

"Mum's being calling me Dante on TV, hasn't she? I wish she'd stop doing that. I keep telling her to call me Dan. I thought she'd finally got used to it."

"I wouldn't know."

"Then how did you know that's my name?"

The flame touched her fingertips and she dropped the match. It went out before it hit the floor. "I dreamt it. Along with Cricket." She was glad for the dark, not sure she'd have been able to mention her dream if she'd been staring into his eyes.

There was silence for a moment before he spoke. "Is he okay? I was taking him for a walk when they grabbed me."

"He's outside." She wished he'd stop talking. She needed to figure out how to escape, not answer his questions. She nearly told him to be quiet again.

"He followed me?"

She lit another match. "I have no idea. All I know is he's outside. He led me to your window." Her heart lurched at the smile he gave her and she tried to slow it down. She had to focus on getting out of here, not admiring Dante. She hissed when the flame reached her fingers again. Letting it drop, she glared at the matches she couldn't see in the dark. Not much of a hunter. Twice she'd burned herself. "We've got to get out of here before they get back."

He moved his hand that was chained to hers. "A bit hard at the moment. You shouldn't have stopped me before."

She drew her hand closer to herself, his coming

with hers, so she could light another match. There had to be something she could light before she ran out of matches. Her gaze landed on the bed. There'd been flames on the bed in her dream. She shook the match out before she burned herself again and stepped forward before she lit another one.

"What are you doing?" Dante tried to stop her.

"Don't. I know what I'm doing." She was glad Essence wasn't there to call her on her lie.

"Are you sure?" He stared at the flames that were flickering in the folds of the sheet.

"Of course. I'm a hunter."

"I thought you said that's your name."

"It's both." As soon as she was happy with the light from the fire on the bed, she took out the case of lock picks, opening it up.

Chapter Five

"Where did you get them from?" Dante gestured towards the lock picks.

"My father." Emily was tempted to tell him to be quiet. There were some questions she'd rather not answer.

"What kind of father gives his daughter lock picks?"

She glared at him before choosing the tools she needed. "The kind who teaches his daughter the skills she needs to survive." Her father's brothers had helped teach her, laughing at her first attempts. The padlock opened and she put away her lock picks, leaving Dante to deal with the chain.

"Sorry."

Even though they should be leaving, she stared at him for a second, but couldn't figure out why he'd said that. "What are you sorry for?"

"Your father is a genius. We might actually get out of here."

"Was." She turned away from him, scanning the room again. They had to get out soon, smoke was starting to fill the room near the ceiling. She tried the window. It was nailed shut. Grabbing the padlock, she threw it at the glass. It took several throws before the glass was broken enough to get through. The moment it broke, air rushed into the room and the flames leapt across the bed. "Don't cut yourself." She climbed carefully out the window, not about to leave any of her blood behind for a demon to consume.

"I don't think a few more cuts are going to make much of a difference."

"They will. The more of your blood they have, the more power it will give them." Although maybe that would be a good thing when it came to Essence. Demons that could hunt during the day were hard to avoid. "Hurry up."

"You told me to be careful." He finished climbing through the window and stopped beside her. "Now what?"

"Be quiet and follow." Before they could move away, a shadow darted towards them. She tensed, relaxing slightly when she realised it was Cricket.

Again. That dog wasn't good for her health. Her heart continued to race.

Dante crouched to throw his arms around the dog. "I missed you too, boy. How did you find me?"

"Quiet." She glared at him even though she doubted he'd be able to see. "Do you want to be caught?"

With one last pat, Dante rose to his feet, Cricket leaning against his leg. "Lead on."

She glanced around the area and, hoping they were still safe, headed for the corner of the house. Peering around she saw it was clear. Her gaze was drawn to her bow and arrows on the ground. Her heart lurched. Was it a trap? Another search of the area showed everything remained clear. "Wait here."

Dante grabbed her arm before she could move away from him. "What are you doing?"

"Getting my weapon. But it could be a trap. If it is, get out of here. Call my family. Leo Hunter is in the phone directory." She pulled out of his grip, darting along the side of the house before he could stop her. She looked around once more before she bent and grabbed her bow and quiver, leaving the arrows that were lying on the ground. A glance towards the back corner showed Dante waited for her. Changing her mind about returning to him, she hurried along the house to check out the front.

Her heart plummeted. A shadowy figure stood on guard, a demon from the way her demon mark burned slightly. One that would vanish with the day. She eased back, making sure he hadn't seen her before she turned away and ran along the side of the house. There were three demons. Hopefully no more, but she didn't like her chances. She thought of and discarded several plans, her gaze continually scanning the surroundings as she listened to every sound.

Dante grabbed hold of her arms when she reached him. "What were you doing? You said it might be a trap. Are you crazy?"

She tilted her head slightly as she looked at him. "I'm not sure. It's always possible."

He let go of her, stepping back. "What do you mean you're not sure?"

She almost laughed and that surprised her. There hadn't been a lot to laugh about lately. "They wanted to do a psych evaluation, but I refused. I quit instead." She looked past him to the smoke billowing out the window. "Let's get out of here before someone finds us." One of the neighbours was sure to notice the fire eventually and call emergency. She strode towards the back fence, slinging her quiver over her head and arm so it sat on her back and doing the same with her bow. She dreaded to think how she'd explain to the police what she was doing walking around with a weapon, late at night, in a Brisbane suburb. She'd rather face a demon.

Dante fell into step beside her, Cricket on his other side. "Have you got a phone?"

"Not on me." She shouldn't have left it in her vehicle, but she'd been worried it would ring or vibrate and draw someone's attention. Some demons had acute hearing. It hadn't mattered. She'd caught their attention anyway. She looked behind. It was all clear. Maybe they could circle around the block and come at her vehicle from the end of the street.

"What's the plan? Why don't we ask for help at one of these houses? We should be banging on someone's door and demanding they called the police."

"And do what? Wait around for the police who probably won't reach us before the demons do?"

"There has to be something we can do. And why aren't we running?"

"We are doing something. We're getting out of here." She reached the metre high back fence and vaulted over it, ignoring the second question. "Did you want to hand me Cricket?"

"Not necessary." He tapped the metal bar that ran

across the top of the fence to hold up the chain wire. "Up, boy."

Cricket jumped onto the fence, his feet barely touching it before he was over the other side, looking at Dante as if to ask what was taking him so long.

Emily patted Cricket on the head. "Clever."

Dante vaulted the fence. "I've done some agility training with him. His mum was an Australian Terrier. I have no idea what his father was, but Australian Terriers are known for their agility." He looked down at Cricket with a smile. "And their loyalty."

She'd already figured out that much of the dog's parentage herself. "How long have you had him?" Talking about the dog might take Dante's mind off the situation.

"Since he was old enough to leave his mum. He's three now." He followed her along the side of the house. "Where are we going?"

There went that plan. Expecting to distract him had probably been an undertaking doomed to failure. "Does it matter?" She had no idea. She was still trying to figure that out herself.

"Yeah. I need to let my family know I'm okay."

She glanced towards him, wondering if she should

tell him how far from safe he really was. Remaining silent, she kept walking.

"What's wrong?"

"What makes you ask that?"

"The look you gave me."

"It's dark."

"Not that dark. There are streetlights."

She hated to have to tell him. Especially after all he must have gone through. "Who cut you?"

"What?"

She gestured towards his chest, pausing before she stepped out onto the footpath, almost wishing there were no streetlights. They made her feel too exposed. "The blood on you."

"What has that got to do with the look you gave me?"

He was so clueless it was scary. "Humour me."

"The demon who chained us together."

"What did he do with the blood? Other than get it all over you?" She nearly said the words, 'like a little kid finger painting'.

"He drank some of it."

That's what she'd feared. "You felt pain when he consumed it?"

"Yeah."

"You have a blood tie with him."

"What's that supposed to mean?"

She glanced towards him before she spoke. "He'll be able to find you. Day or night. Unless his power grows so he can't be about during the day." Her gaze was drawn to every sound and there were far too many, keeping her heart racing and having her want to run.

"What about my family?"

She had no idea what to say. Obviously the whole world knew who they were since their faces had been plastered all over the television.

"Emily?" He waited until she glanced towards him before he spoke again. "What about my family?"

"I don't know."

Stopping, he grabbed hold of her shoulders and spun her to face him. "What do you mean you don't know? How do I keep them from going after my family? My sister, Jane, is only eleven. Heathcliff, my brother, is fifteen. Am I meant to let the demons get them?"

She pulled out of his grip, half tempted to comment on the names his parents had chosen. "We can't do anything until we get away."

"Then why aren't we doing something other than calmly walking down the street? Can you hotwire a car?"

There were some things she'd rather avoid doing, even though she could. "I have a vehicle parked on their street. And you're not very calm."

"Why didn't you tell me? Where is it? And why aren't we moving quicker? I've asked you that several times."

And she'd avoided answering several times rather than panicking him further. "Because we need to keep an eye out for demons. As soon as they notice the fire they will be after us." She paused at the corner, looking up the street. It seemed clear, but that didn't mean anything with the amount of shadows that things could be hidden in. She rubbed at her demon mark. It seemed fine, no itching or anything to indicate there was a demon nearby.

"What's that?" Dante gestured towards her wrist.

"Demon mark."

"You're a demon?"

Deciding it was as safe as possible, she started walking down the next street. "No. It's from fighting them." It was a wonder that demons hadn't taken over the world by now with how clueless most people were about them. Reaching the next corner, she paused again. There was her vehicle. No one seemed to be near it. Yet she couldn't bring herself to move.

"Why are we standing here?"

She turned to Dante. Cricket was leaning against his leg again. "Demons move faster than us. They're also stronger."

"And?"

"Taking them out from a distance is our best chance of beating one."

Dante gestured towards her bow. "You can kill them with that?"

"Not exactly." She slipped it over her head, feeling a little better with it in her hand. She left the arrows in her quiver so she'd have a free hand to get the keys from under the vehicle.

"Then what's the use of it?"

There wasn't a simple answer. "Stay behind me." She headed for her vehicle, her gaze continually drawn to where the house was, unable to see the area in front of it because of the broken streetlight. The next streetlight along shone light on the side of the house and she tried to see if there was anyone or anything there. She wasn't close enough to tell. How long was it until daylight? Not that it'd help with Essence. He'd still be able to come after them and track Dante down.

Chapter Six

"Why are you helping me?"

Emily glanced at Dante. "What?"

"You risked your life for me. Why?"

It had been months since she'd been willing to risk death for a stranger. Even longer since someone had asked her why. "Habit." It was the first word she'd thought of, others coming to mind the moment she'd spoken it. But none of them were as accurate.

Dante chuckled, a startled note to it as if her words had surprised it from him. "No wonder you fear for your sanity."

"That's a different matter altogether." She reached the vehicle, her gaze scanning the area before she bent to collect the keys. She'd barely managed to retrieve them before she felt the demon coming. It was the one that had been guarding the front of the house. He was coming in too quick. She tossed the keys to Dante. "Get it started and turned around." She drew an arrow from the quiver, waiting for the demon to be close enough.

"What–"

"Not now." Her tone was sharp. "Start the vehicle before it's too late." She fired the arrow, the demon roaring. She rapidly sent more arrows after him, wishing Dante would hurry up before she ran out of ammunition. She had four arrows left. The demon recovered enough to head towards her again and she fired another two arrows. Relief rushed through her at the sound of the engine starting. When the demon came towards her, she fired one more arrow. She reached for the last arrow, waiting. Holding her breath, she watched as the demon ripped the arrow from his body, clawing at the wound that probably burned from the holy water. She mentally urged Dante to hurry.

He finished turning the vehicle around and reversed up to her. The driver's window was down. "Get in."

She wasn't crazy enough to argue. Firing the last arrow at the demon, she got in the back of the four-wheel-drive, Cricket on the seat beside her. "Go." She closed her door.

"Where to?"

"Just go. We'll worry about that later." She leaned over the back seat and opened the weapon box, taking out some of the arrows lying loosely in the bottom. She refilled her quiver, after removing it from her back to make it easier to sit. Leaving it on the floor leaning against the seat with her bow, she climbed between the front seats to sit beside Dante. "Head for the highway and stick to the speed limit for now. We need to put some distance between them and us and being pulled over by the police won't help."

"What about my family?"

"I'll take care of that."

"How?"

She took her phone from her satchel, seeing the many missed calls from her grandparents and Leo. She'd let Leo talk to them. Dialling his number, she glanced towards Dante. She'd once known why she fought demons. Now she wasn't so sure if there was a reason other than habit. That word scared her more than the demons had. She didn't want her life to be nothing but a habit.

"Emily? Where are you? Do you need help?"

She hadn't even thought to check the time. It must be late with the fear she could hear in Leo's voice. "Yes. I do need help."

"Then it's yours. What can we do?"

The reassurance in his tone brought a slight smile to her lips and an ache to her throat. "You know the missing boy that's been all over the news?"

"Dan Mills?"

"Yeah." She guessed he'd be happy to know his mother wasn't telling everyone his name was Dante. "I found him." She told Leo everything. Apart from dreaming about her parents' death. She couldn't talk about that yet. He was silent for a moment when she finished.

"I'll send the boys for his family. They can bring them here, but that'll mean you'll have to take him elsewhere."

She almost smiled at the way he always called his brothers boys even though Adam, the youngest, was in his late thirties. "I know." She would have anyway. They didn't need demons camping on their doorstep.

"Is there something the boys can tell his family so they'll know he's sent them?"

"I'll ask." She muted her phone while she did.

"Will they be safe with your family?"

"Yeah. My family have been trained to deal with things like this. We've been fighting demons for generations."

He was silent a moment. "The Guide and I into

that hidden road now entered, to return to the bright world."

"Dante's Inferno?"

"Yeah. Mum often quotes it to me. She keeps telling me there's a quote for nearly every occasion. Tell them to say I'm no longer with those who were holding me. I had help getting away. Make sure they say exactly that or the quote won't mean anything to her."

"Okay." She relayed his message.

"What do you plan to do, Emily?"

She had no answers for Leo. "I don't know. I'm still working that out. Do you think you could ring my grandparents?"

"Have you considered they might deserve a call from you themselves?"

"Please, Uncle Leo? I can't-" she broke off, not wanting to explain things while Dante listened.

"They'll probably ring you."

"Ask them not to. Give me at least a day." Longer would be better. There were things she needed to figure out and they were sure to have questions she couldn't answer yet.

"I'll see what I can do. I'm not much of a miracle worker."

She half smiled at his dry tone of voice. "Thank you."

"Let me know when you figure out what you're doing."

"I will."

"Be careful."

She frowned at the worry she could hear in his voice. "What do you know?"

"The family has been investigating Eternally Flawless Beauty Cream for a while."

His cautious tone made her pause, her worry increasing. Not from what they'd been investigating, but who'd been doing the investigating. "Who?"

"Several family members including Aunt Louise."

She couldn't stop herself asking. "Mum and Dad?"

"Why don't we talk about this later?"

"Were they?" There was a sharpness to her voice and she noticed Dante glance at her.

Leo was silent for a moment. "Your parents followed the trail from Mackay to Brisbane, but the night they died they were out on another matter. We didn't lie to you about what happened. We'd never do that. They witnessed a random attack by a demon and followed him to the house where they were ambushed."

"Okay. I'll talk to you later." When she ended the

call, she stared out the window, trying to work out where they were rather than think about the conversation with Leo. Not far from the motorway. Closing her eyes, she rubbed her demon mark, trying to focus on it. There seemed to be no demons nearby. Or at least no major ones.

"What do we do now?"

She stared out the window for a few more seconds before she looked at Dante. "Are you okay to drive? Not too tired?"

"I can drive. For now. What's the plan?"

She had none, other than to stay alive. The blood-splattered room came to mind. Thinking about that wasn't going to help. "Keep moving. If we keep moving they might not be able to catch us."

"You said you dreamt about me and Cricket."

"Yeah." She could hear it in his voice that he'd been hoping she'd give him more of an answer than that. More than he would have heard during her conversation with Leo.

"Is that normal? For a hunter?"

She continued to stare at him, meeting his gaze when he momentarily looked towards her. "No."

He glanced towards her again. "You don't say much, do you?"

She used to, once upon a time. Before she let her

parents die there'd been many days when she'd spent hours chatting to friends on the phone, talking to her family and rehashing old battles at Hunter family gatherings. "No."

"How do I stop this?"

She tilted her head on a slight angle unable to figure out what he meant. "Stop what?"

"The demons you said would come after me. And my family."

She thought of Susan and the beauty cream. Eternally Flawless. "We need more information."

"How do we get that?"

She didn't bother to answer, using her phone to search the internet, wishing she had her glasses. There was a surprising amount of information about Susan Lunsford and Eternally Flawless, the miracle beauty cream that had the fifty-year-old woman looking like she was in her late twenties. She couldn't believe people were paying a thousand dollars for a small jar of Eternally Flawless.

"Did you find anything useful?"

"No."

He sighed loud enough Emily could hear him. "Why don't you tell me what you did find?"

It was Emily's turn to sigh. When had working with people become so difficult? There'd once been so much laughter in her life. Laughter and excitement. The thrill of the hunt, tracking down demons and when they'd done wrong, returning them to hell. She'd been on so many hunts learning how to defeat demons. And she'd loved it. Every single minute. Until that night six months ago when she hadn't gone hunting and her parents hadn't come home.

She closed her eyes. She'd almost gone with them. But she'd promised her friend she'd be there for her birthday and she couldn't be in two towns at once. She'd resented her for a time, partly blaming her. If she'd gone with her parents, would it have made a difference? Images from her dream flickered through her mind. Three of them wouldn't have helped. There'd been too many. The demon had led them into a trap. No matter how many times everyone told her it was a random attack, she hadn't believed them. Not after what she'd seen in her dream. Now she knew the dream had probably been real, she had to tell someone. But not yet. She needed some time to take it all in first.

"You okay?"

She opened her eyes, looking towards Dante. "I don't know." She was sick of saying yes when it clearly wasn't true.

"Can I help?"

She stared at him. There was some dried blood smeared across his jaw and shadows under his eyes. A closer look showed how tense he was, his knuckles white from his grip on the steering wheel. She should have realised he probably wasn't as calm as he was acting. "No. Do you want me to drive?"

He hesitated a moment then shook his head. "It gives me something to focus on." He was silent a moment before he spoke again. "Do you ever wonder if you're going crazy?"

She couldn't stop a slight smile from forming. "All the time."

He glanced towards her. "How do you know if you are?"

"You don't."

"Demons shouldn't exist." He slowly shook his head. "Do you know how ironic it was to end up there with a name like mine?"

"What made your mum call you that?" Anything had to be a better topic than talking about sanity, or lack of it.

"She was going through a medieval poet stage. I guess I should be grateful she didn't name me after Perceval Doria or Ulrich von Türheim. She has their work too."

"I guess your brother is named for Heathcliff in Wuthering Heights." At his nod, she continued. "How did your sister end up with a normal name?"

"Most people think that, but she didn't really. She's named for Jane Austen. Not that she's happy about it. She reckons it's not fair we got the interesting names while she was stuck with the boring one. Mum said she can always change her name too when she turns eighteen."

"Too?"

"Mum changed her name to Rainbow."

"Oh." She had no idea what to say.

Dante chuckled. "That's a pretty typical response." He glanced towards her again. "How long are we going to drive around?"

"Until I figure out a plan." Or someone else does. As soon as they stopped the demon would track them down.

"What are the options?"

Chapter Seven

Emily couldn't think of a single option so she didn't bother answering Dante's question. "Did you see who held you, other than the demons?"

He shook his head. "I heard what you said to your uncle though."

"She can't let me live. I could ruin all her plans, whatever they are."

"What about me?"

She eyed him carefully, not sure if he was up to any more bad news. "She'll assume I've told you everything."

He remained silent a moment. "She'll need to kill me too, won't she?"

Emily continued to watch him carefully. Maybe she should have suggested he pull over first. "Yeah." Her voice was soft, little more than a whisper.

Dante kept his gaze on the road ahead, his knuckles

still white from how tight he gripped the steering wheel. "How do we stop her?"

And they were back to her original dilemma of no plan. Her phone rang and she nearly cheered at the interruption. At least until she saw it was Leo. "Yes?" Her voice was hesitant.

"Are you still with Dan?"

"Yeah."

"His mother would like to speak to him. She wants to hear for herself that he's okay."

"I'll put the phone on speaker. He's driving."

"Emily."

She'd been about to take the phone away from her ear so she could see to put it on speaker mode. "Yes?"

"I rang Gran and told her everything."

She didn't bother correcting him that he couldn't have. She hadn't told him everything. "Okay."

"She said she'd be ringing you soon."

She wanted to demand why. "Okay."

"You can put the phone on speaker now."

Instead of answering, she changed the mode before saying anything. "You're on speaker."

"I'll put Rainbow on the phone."

There was a moment of silence before a woman spoke. "Dan?" Her voice was hesitant.

"I'm here, Mum."

Again there was silence and what might have been a sob. "When will I see you?"

"I'm not sure."

"They said you're being kept in protective custody until those who kidnapped you have been apprehended."

"Yeah." He swallowed audibly. "I have to go, Mum. I'll talk to you later. Tomorrow or something."

The sob was clear this time. "Are you okay? Did they hurt you?"

"They didn't get a chance to do anything. I have to go. Bye, Mum." He reached out and disconnected the call.

Emily dropped her phone into the satchel, not sure what to say.

Dante pulled off onto the side of the motorway, in a breakdown lane under a streetlight. He turned off the engine.

"Dante?"

He didn't answer, getting out he paced back and forth a couple of times before stopping in front of the bonnet and resting his hands on the bulbar, leaning heavily on them.

Cricket whined and she looked towards the dog. She had no answers for him either. Looking away, she stared at Dante through the windscreen, wondering if she should get out. She watched as he pushed away from the bulbar, turning his back on her to run his hands through his hair. She sighed. It would be wrong to leave him out there alone. He faced her direction when she opened the door, closing it behind her. "We can't stay in one place for long." She rubbed her demon mark. There were none nearby. Not yet anyway.

He ran his hands through his hair again. "What do I tell her?"

She moved closer to him. "About what?"

"Everything. I didn't realise they'd lie to her. I know it's probably weird, but we don't lie to Mum. None of us do. There's no reason to."

"You can tell her whatever you want. Most people can't handle the truth though."

He turned away from her, swearing. "I keep thinking it's a nightmare. Something I should be able to wake up from."

She laughed, a harsh sound she'd only learned in the past six months. "Nightmares are worse than this. Someone always dies in them."

He faced her at her words. "It isn't over yet."

She could see the fear in his eyes and in the way he held his body. She reached for him, taking his hand like she'd done earlier, when the demon had chained them together. "I won't let them kill you."

"Why? I'm nothing to you. Why would you care if I lived or died?"

"Nothing? Then why did I dream of you?" And why had she felt like she'd known him right from the moment she'd first seen him in her dream? She had as many unanswered questions as he did.

"I don't know, why did you?"

He would have to ask that. "So I could save you."

"But why? Why me?"

His words were so close to her own. She was nothing special to be given premonitions. He obviously thought the same. Reaching out, she tried to clean the smudge of blood from his jaw. It remained. "I guess you're more important than you think." An itch started in her demon mark. "Get in the vehicle. I'm driving." Releasing him, she strode around to the driver's door, relieved when he moved equally as fast.

He got in as she started the engine. "What's going on?"

"There's a demon in the area. I can feel him."

"How?"

After pulling back out onto the motorway, she held out her arm, the demon mark in front of his eyes.

She glanced at him when he brushed his fingers over her wrist. "I can sense demons in the area. But they can also sense me." She drew her arm away from him, putting her hand on the steering wheel. "If they're strong enough."

"How close?"

"It doesn't work like that. I'd have to know if it was a major or minor demon to judge that with any accuracy. A major demon at a distance feels like a minor demon up close."

"Will I end up with one of those?" He indicated her wrist.

"That depends on how involved you are in getting rid of your demons."

He laughed, a sound very similar to the sharp one she'd made earlier.

"What?" She glanced in the rear view mirror. She could see nothing, but she could still feel the demon through her mark.

"Most people don't mean real demons when they make that comment."

She reluctantly smiled. "I guess not."

He became serious. "I don't care what it takes. I want to be involved in getting rid of them."

"Okay." She could understand that. She wanted to take Essence and Flawless down too. She hated feeling powerless. If she knew how to find the demons who'd killed her parents, she'd also send them to hell now she knew she wouldn't freeze when facing one.

"What are we going to do?"

"Dante-"

"Why do you keep calling me that?"

"It's the name I was given." He'd heard her explanation to Leo, surely he could understand. "Why do you keep asking me what the plan is?"

"Everyone calls me Dan."

She glanced towards him, a half smile forming. "I'm not everyone."

He was silent for nearly a minute before he answered. "No, you're not." His next silence was shorter. "You haven't told me our plan yet."

"I don't have one."

"We can't keep driving around in circles."

She clamped her teeth together rather than snap at him. Her phone ringing nearly had her cheering again. When he handed it to her, she hit the speaker button, wondering if she'd been relieved too soon. "You're on speaker, Gran."

"I need to see you, child."

"There's a demon following us. Maybe two."

"How does Dante feel about blood samples and transfusions?"

"Are you laying a false trail so he can hide for a couple of days?"

"And setting a trap."

Emily glanced towards Dante. "What do you think?"

"Not much. You haven't really explained anything."

"Someone will take blood. Enough to figure out your blood type and fill several vials. They'll take them in different directions, a group of hunters with each vial. You'll be given a blood transfusion that will hide your blood from the demon who has a blood tie with you. It's not something we use often since we never have much blood stored and we tend to keep it for those who really need it," Emily said.

"Why would you store blood?"

"Because medical staff start to wonder and ask questions if the same person tends to frequently need medical help. And that leads to the sort of attention we don't need." She glanced towards him, willing him to say yes. She was getting sick of driving.

"Is it safe?"

"Nothing about demons is safe."

"I think he is asking about the blood, child."

She felt her cheeks heat at Gran's comment. "Of course it's safe. It's for our family."

"Okay. I'll do it. Will I get to be at one of the traps?"

"We will see what happens," Gran said.

She nearly told him that was probably a definite no. "Where should we go to?"

"How close is the demon?"

"I haven't seen him yet."

"Leo will let you know where to meet up. This might be best done in stages and keeping you on the move until Dante has camouflage."

"Okay."

Dante didn't speak again until Gran had hung up. "Is all your family going to call me Dante?"

"Probably not. But Gran rarely shortens people's names."

"Will this work?"

"It has before."

"Then will I be able to go home?"

Why did he keep asking her difficult questions? "The demons are only part of the problem." Her phone beeped. She glanced at the address. "Can you put that in the GPS?

He did so without comment. It wasn't until he'd

finished that he spoke. "Who will give me a transfusion?"

"A doctor." When she glanced at him, she nearly laughed at his expression. "We don't only hunt demons. The pay for that is lousy."

"You get paid for hunting demons?"

She chuckled. It was a family joke. "Not exactly." She checked the GPS to see when she needed to get off the motorway. It would be soon.

Dante fell silent, staring out the window. He didn't speak again until they pulled up in a quiet street behind another four-wheel-drive. "Are they planning on taking much?"

She watched two people get out of the vehicle, one of them Gran's youngest daughter, Louise, who was a doctor. She had salt and pepper hair and was in her late sixties. The other person who walked towards them was Louise's oldest son, Carl. He also was a doctor. At thirty-seven his black hair was silvering at the sides, having started to go grey in his early twenties. She almost smiled as she remembered how the family had teased him about it. She turned to Dante. "What's wrong?" He'd sounded worried. More worried them before.

"I have no idea how much I've already lost." He

looked down at his body. "I didn't make it easy for him to take it."

She'd guessed there must have been a fight. Most people didn't stay still when a demon was slicing into them with claws. Although some did. "You'll be getting a transfusion soon. I wouldn't worry about it. Blood always looks like far more than is actually spilled." The house in her nightmares came to mind. That wasn't a good example. Far too much had been shed.

Chapter Eight

Louise swung the passenger door open. "I'm Louise and this is my son, Carl. I guess you're Dan." At his nod, she continued. "We don't have long to do this. I can feel a demon coming."

"He's been following us." Emily watched as Louise prepared everything with the help of Carl.

Louise remained standing beside Dante, taking the needle Carl handed her, having already cleaned Dante's arm. "Are you ready?"

Dante nodded, looking away.

Emily met his gaze, reaching for his free hand and lightly squeezing it. "It won't take long."

"When I know his blood type, and it's after sunrise, I'll meet you on the road." Louise peered in the back seat. "I can set him up in there for his transfusion."

"While Emily is driving around?" Dante asked.

"Yes." Louise looked away. "I'll let you go. He's

very close now." She gathered her gear and strode away.

Emily didn't hesitate. She pulled out onto the street the moment the door was closed. The demon wasn't minor. She could feel the burn in her wrist. It didn't matter. The moment sunrise arrived he'd be gone until dark. If they were lucky only Essence would be minor enough to remain and they should be able to easily deal with him.

Silence filled the vehicle for several minutes, eventually broken by Dante. "How do you cope with it? Or understand. Demons shouldn't exist. It's like I've stepped into a horror movie. One that it's impossible to escape. And I don't know who the hero of the movie is or if I'll survive. I've got a bad feeling I'm only the sidekick and they never fare well in horror movies."

She had no idea what to say to that comment. Everything seemed condescending. These days she struggled to come up with phrases for ordinary conversations. She remained silent. It seemed like the best option. Checking her rear view mirror, her heart leapt and she took the next corner fast.

Dante grabbed the roof handle above his window. "What are you doing?"

"They're behind us."

"Who?" He turned to look out the back, swearing. "Aren't they worried other people will see Essence?"

"I doubt it. He's probably hidden from the average person. I'm more worried about Susan. She's got a gun. And Flawless. He's more powerful than Essence." Although the fact Essence could steal their lives, if he came close enough to touch, was a concern.

"What about that life stealing thing Essence said he could do?"

He would have to ask about that. She took another corner fast, wishing she was back home where she knew the streets. "He needs to be close enough to touch." She glanced towards him. "All we have to do is keep a little ahead of them. They're going to have to stop before dawn because Flawless is driving."

"Why will they?"

"He'll disappear. He's too powerful to be about in the daylight. If they don't pull over, they'll crash." She looked at the time displayed on the dash. About half an hour. She could do that. Catching up to a car going slower than her, she slipped around it, narrowly missing an oncoming vehicle, ignoring the driver who hit the horn repeatedly.

"I thought you said you didn't want to be pulled over by the cops."

"I don't, but I want to be caught by Susan even less."

"What happens if the cops try and pull us over?"

She glanced at him, a half smile forming. "You really don't want to know." A high-speed car chase with the police would probably see them behind bars. She slipped around another car, checking the mirror to find she'd put some distance between them. Not enough.

Cricket whined and Dante reached out to pat him. "It's okay, boy."

She could hear it in his voice that he didn't believe his own words. She doubted Cricket believed him either. Before she could say anything, a parked car slid out in front of them and she hit the brakes, narrowly missing running into it as she went to the left of the car, the wheels of her vehicle going over the edge of the footpath. If the police noticed her, she'd probably lose her licence. Better that than her life. Although ending up imprisoned would make it easy for demons to get her.

"How did that happen? There was no one in it."

"Demon." A glance showed her he was once again white-knuckled. She didn't blame him. "I've been taught defensive driving and some techniques by a stunt driver."

"That doesn't make me feel any better," Dante muttered.

"It should do. It means we have a higher than average chance of getting out of this alive." And she did feel alive. It was the first time in months she'd felt that way. How had she thought she could give this up? An image came to her of fighting at her parents' sides and some of the fierce joy left her. She pushed it away. They would have been disappointed to see how she'd been letting life drift by. Especially her father. If anyone had thrown himself into life and all it offered, it had been him.

Ahead was a set of traffic lights. They were red. She didn't slow. Susan was too close.

"What are you doing?"

She couldn't miss the fear in his voice. She didn't blame him, not with the cars regularly crossing in front of them. Holding her breath, her grip tightened on the steering wheel as she looked for a gap. Choosing one, she sped up.

"Emily!"

She couldn't answer. Her attention was focused on the gap. Then she was through it and hitting the brakes as the car ahead of her came closer, another one oncoming. Behind was the squeal of tires and numerous horns. She turned the steering wheel to the right, slipping around the car in front once the oncoming vehicle had passed, her heart going faster than her vehicle. They needed to get back on a motorway, or the highway. Somewhere without traffic lights. "Put Mackay in the GPS for me." It was the first place that came to mind. Home. She'd have to return eventually. She needed to see her grandparents. There were things she had to say. The dream came to mind. Apologies to make.

"I don't know if I can let go long enough to do that." He clung to the edge of his seat and the handle above the window.

She laughed, equal parts humour and surprise. "You'll manage."

"Is that where we're going?"

"No. But we need to get out of this traffic." Her phone rang and she breathed out heavily. "Think you can get that?"

"GPS or phone? I can't do both." He continued to hold onto the handle while he keyed the town into the GPS.

"They'll ring back." She looked at the time. Fifteen minutes. A glance in the mirror showed more space between them. Flawless was going to have to pull over soon.

The phone rang again and Dante answered it, putting it on speaker.

"We've been tracking your phone and have a location to meet you at sunrise," Leo said.

"Who?" Emily checked the mirror. This time they'd gained on her.

"Louise and Carl again."

"Okay. What then?"

"As soon as Dan has had his transfusion and you've lost your tail, you need to see Gran. She's waiting for you."

She didn't know if she was up to speaking to Gran. "Okay."

"Are you ready for the location?" Leo asked.

Emily glanced at Dante. "Put it in the GPS, please?" When he nodded, she said, "Go ahead, Uncle Leo." Another look in the mirror showed Susan was closer. While Dante put in the new address, she checked the time. Flawless would have to stop soon. She pressed down a little more on the accelerator. It was Sunday morning. All the people on the road could have been considerate enough to sleep in.

"You take care, Emily. Go with God."

"You too, Uncle."

When Dante disconnected the call, he looked at her for a moment. "You're religious?"

She couldn't resist another smile. "You say that like you're asking me if I'm contagious."

"Are you?"

"Contagious?" She couldn't resist.

"Religious."

"Let's just say it's hard not to believe when you've spent your entire life knowing demons exist and learning how to fight them."

Dante looked over his shoulder, still clinging to the handle. "I thought you said they'd have to pull over."

"They will." She checked the time. "Any minute now. Either that or there's going to be a spectacular car accident behind us. Somehow I don't think Susan will allow that."

"Why aren't they slowing?"

She glanced in the mirror. "I don't know, but she's cutting it close." Surely they'd have to stop. She'd been certain Flawless was powerful enough he couldn't stay in the daylight. The burn in her demon mark told her that. Unless it was like that because the two of them were following. She pushed aside her doubts, trying to remind herself she'd felt the burn when she'd first seen Flawless. But she hadn't known Essence was in the area too. She kept checking her mirror, reminding herself to breathe when the car following gained on her. She nearly cheered when the car pulled over, relief rushing through her.

Dante continued to stare out the back window as the sun rose. "I thought they were never going to stop. Will we be able to lose them now?"

"We don't need to lose them yet, just get far enough ahead to be able to pick up Louise and Carl."

"I'm not going to have a blood transfusion in the middle of a car chase."

This time it was a grin that broke free. The last time she'd found anything even the slightest bit amusing had been more than six months ago. As crazy as it had been, as well as scary and that there'd been moments when she'd thought she might die, she'd needed this. Needed to learn she was still capable of hunting.

"Are you laughing at me?"

"Not really."

"Are you sure?" His voice was filled with suspicion and his eyes were narrowed. He continued to hold onto the handle above the window.

"More the situation than you." She tried to send him a reassuring smile. She wasn't sure she managed. "Louise will only give you the transfusion if it's safe."

"None of this seems very safe."

She couldn't argue with that comment. There was

very little about demons that was safe. When he turned his attention to Cricket, reassuring the dog that whined again, she was relieved. They remained silent until they reached the meeting point and she pulled over, still having no clue what to tell him.

Louise opened the back door. "In the back, Dan. Can the dog sit in the front?"

Emily nodded, watching as Louise rearranged everyone, Carl getting in on the other side of Dante. She kept glancing in the rear view mirror, hoping they'd put enough distance between them. As soon as Louise had the transfusion started, Emily pulled back out onto the road. Whoever was driving Louise's vehicle followed behind them, gradually dropping back.

"How long will this take?" Dante asked.

"A trip to the city." Louise paused. "Take the next left, Emily."

"Is this safe?" Dante asked.

Chapter Nine

Emily half listened as Louise explained about screening and full blood transfusions compared to separated blood, giving the occasional direction on where to turn. Susan hadn't caught up to them by the time she reached the city and she wondered why. She pulled into a multi-storey car park. "I haven't seen Susan since they had to pull over."

"We had several people drop in behind us with the vials of blood. They all headed off in different directions after about twenty minutes. Find a park on the third level." Louise started packing everything away with the help of Carl.

Emily found a park on the third level, giving her key to Carl when he held out his hand. Before she could ask what was happening next, she saw Alex, one of her relatives she called cousin, headed towards her. She turned to Dante who stood beside her,

Cricket leaning against his leg. "If you think I drive bad then you don't want to be in a vehicle with him during a car chase."

Alex grinned fleetingly, reaching them in time to hear her words. He held out his hand. "I'm Alex Hunter." His dark brown hair was so short it was almost shaved. He had a square jaw, sharp cheekbones, deep brown eyes, a solemn look and broad shoulders.

Dante took the offered hand. "Dan Mills."

Alex looked from one to the other. "Ready to go?"

"One minute." Emily grabbed her satchel, slipping her phone back in it. She hesitated over her bow and arrows.

"Leave them," Louise said. "We'll get your vehicle over to Mum's place when we're absolutely certain it's no longer being followed."

It always felt odd hearing Gran referred to by any other name. She nodded, closing the door, surprised by how difficult she found it to leave her bow behind. She walked beside Alex. Dante and Cricket walked on the other side of her. "How is your sister, Alex?"

"Getting there."

She knew that feeling. "Is there anyone else at Gran's?"

Alex shrugged. "I don't know. I haven't been over

there today." Using the central locking button on his key he unlocked the four-wheel-drive they approached.

She guessed she'd have to wait and see, but she really wanted to talk to Gran on her own. She doubted it was something she could talk about while others were listening. When Dante got in the back seat, she got in the front. The trip to Gran's place was silent and she was relieved. She had no idea what to talk about after having said so little during the past six months. Exhaustion also dragged at her now she was safe and she wanted to sleep.

Alex pulled up in front of Gran's house, parking beside Louise's vehicle that was in front of the double garage doors. The spacious house was surrounded by flowering gardens and built from timber painted in neutral creams and browns. "I won't stay. I've got other things I need to do today."

Emily swung open the front door, remaining in her seat a moment longer. "Thanks for the lift."

Alex grinned fleetingly. "Any time."

She stood beside Dante and waved to Alex as he drove off. "Come on." Striding to the front door, she didn't check to see if Dante and Cricket followed. Trying the front door, she found it unlocked. Someone was obviously expecting her. She didn't know if she was up to this. How did you tell someone you let your parents die?

She stepped inside an entrance hall. The floor tiles were off-white and the walls a similar cream to outside. There were two closed doors on her left that led to a bathroom and a guest room. On her right she could see the lounge room through an open door and a door straight ahead led to the rest of the house. On either side of the front door were racks hung with coats and hats, and two wooden boxes with a jumble of shoes. The curtains hanging at the narrow windows on either side of the front door were a darker cream than the walls. She left her boots by the front door, noticing Dante did the same.

"What about Cricket? Is it okay to bring him inside?"

Louise stepped out of the lounge room. "She's waiting for you in here, Emily." Her gaze went to Dante. "How about we get you cleaned up?" She gestured towards the bathroom door, smiling. "Cricket is welcome to come too." She started to walk past Emily, but paused instead. "Carl will be here shortly with your four-wheel-drive."

Turning to Dante, Emily saw the uneasiness in his expression. She rested a hand on his arm. "I won't be long." When he nodded, she left him by the door and went into the lounge room. Gran was sitting on an armchair and Emily had to blink back tears at the sight of her. She always looked ageless, like she'd been around forever and would always be around. Her face was lined and full of hollows, her hazel eyes missing nothing. Her grey hair was pulled back and plaited to end past her shoulders and she wore a cross on a thin gold chain.

Gran rose to her feet holding out her arms, her demon mark winding almost to her left shoulder, evenly spaced the entire way. When Emily stepped into her embrace, Gran's arms tightened around her and she patted her gently on the back.

There was something about Gran that always made her feel safe. "I dreamt about them. The night they died."

"I guessed you did when I heard about your recent dream. There's always the first dream. For the one you can't save."

She drew away from Gran. "What do you mean?"

"Come and sit down, child. Let me tell you a story about when I was eleven and my oldest brother was seventeen."

She let Gran lead her to the pale brown lounge suite and sat beside her. The lounge room was both spacious and cosy. The lounge suite was in the middle of the room set around a rustic coffee table with a couple of large, square footstools. Pictures of the family hung in groups on the walls and a long display cabinet filled with ornaments was along another wall. The wall opposite the door was taken up by a floor to ceiling built-in bookcase with glass doors, the shelves full.

Gran reached for Emily's hand, cradling it in hers. "His name was Patrick. It was common in those days to call the firstborn after the father. He was six years older than me and he died the year our last sibling was born." She fell silent for a moment, her eyes losing focus. She shook her head once, her gaze returning to Emily. "I woke screaming, calling for my parents. My mother sent someone after him. It was too late. While I'd been dreaming, it had been happening. There was nothing I could have done. It comes to us from my mother's line. She explained it to me. The first one we can never save, but my mother had tried anyway."

"It was two of them. Not one."

"I know. I know, child." Gran patted her hand. "The first dream, no matter how many are in it, they're the ones you can't save. The second one, if you don't save them, you'll never have another premonition again. If the boy lives you'll be given premonitions in your dreams for the rest of your life. Not every night, but enough to make a difference."

She shook her head even though she knew Gran would be telling her the truth. "What if I can't save them? What if I can't put the pieces of the puzzle together to save anyone?"

"Save who? The boy?"

"No. All of them. The ones in the future. What if I let them die?"

Gran clasped Emily's hand tightly. "Oh, child. It isn't your fault. You can't be expected to save every single one. Some will die. That is the way of life. But the premonitions will give you the chance to save ones that would have otherwise been lost. Even if you save one out of every dozen that is a victory."

"What if I don't want this?"

"Then you let the boy die."

"Gran!" She stared at the woman in front of her, wondering if maybe she'd heard wrong. How could she let Dante die? The pain that arrowed through her was surprising. She barely knew him. An image came to her of Dante standing in front of her, the light from the match flickering between them as he smiled at her. She didn't know him yet, but she wanted to.

Gran chuckled softly. "I knew you didn't have it in you. You're a true Hunter. We were born to protect."

"I'm scared." That was such a mild word for how she felt. Terrified didn't even come close.

Gran patted her hand again. "Of course you are. You're not an idiot. Anyone with an ounce of sense is scared when it comes to demons. You're a Hunter and you'll do what must be done regardless of fear."

She stared into Gran's eyes, slowly nodding as she thought of everything she'd done last night and this morning. Yes, she was a Hunter. In both senses of the word. For a while she'd forgotten that. "I want to bring her down. I want to know if she was responsible for my parents' death. And if not her, I want to know who. They knew they were coming." She slowly shook her head. "Those demons, they knew Mum and Dad were coming. They were led into that room."

"This isn't about revenge?"

She tilted her head to the side, thinking before she answered. "No. This is about people who shouldn't mess with demons." She thought of Susan with her flawless skin and ageless look. How many had died so she could remain beautiful? How many more would be sacrificed so she could remain forever young? "This is about being a Hunter." The last piece of the puzzle clicked into place. How could she have forgotten who she was?

Gran smiled, rising to her feet, drawing Emily up with her. "Let's talk strategy. Your boy should be in the kitchen having breakfast with Louise. And Carl if he's returned. I sent the others away so we didn't overwhelm him."

She smiled fleetingly. They tended to do that when they were in a large group. She walked beside Gran. "We won't find them at the house where Dante was held. They've moved on. At least that's what Susan's plan was."

"I'm not surprised. That's the logical decision. But don't worry about it right now. You look like you need something to eat yourself. And have some sleep." Gran's lips curved into an enigmatic smile. "When all this is over, I'll tell you about the second one I dreamt of. You'll find that story interesting."

She wasn't sure she wanted to know. Not with Gran's expression. They stepped into the kitchen and she smiled at the look of relief Dante quickly masked. She sat beside him, taking the plate of food Carl dished up when he saw her enter the room. While she ate, she checked Dante over. Someone had given him a black long sleeved button up shirt. He looked tired, but had obviously had a shower, getting rid of all signs of blood.

"I've heard back from most of the teams." Louise nursed a cup of coffee, an empty plate in front of her.

"How did they fare?" Gran was seated at the table across from her daughter.

"Neither of the two minor demons that took the bait answered to the name of Essence."

"He's still after me?" Dante asked.

Gran nodded. "Or he will be when he can track your blood again."

"What do I do then? Have another blood transfusion?"

"No." Louise pushed her cup aside, rising to her feet. "We don't have an endless supply."

"If I was injured and lost blood the hospital would have to give me a transfusion," Dante said.

"How would you know when you'd lost enough, to warrant the hospital giving you blood, without killing yourself?" Louise gave him a hard look before turning away to put her dirty dishes in the sink. She faced him again. "They'd most likely give you separated blood and that won't help. Not for your needs."

"What am I supposed to do? Wait for him to get me?"

Chapter Ten

Emily reached for Dante's hand that was on the table, curled into a tight fist. "He would need to go through me first." The thought of him dying wasn't acceptable. It looked like she'd be stuck with premonitions for life. She supposed she better start getting used to them.

"None of us will desert you, Dante. Fighting demons is our calling," Gran said.

"He prefers Dan," Emily said.

Gran gave him a look that clearly said he was lacking in sense. "If you insist, but Dante is such a lovely name."

"I don't mind," Dante said.

Emily bit back a smile. She'd tried, but even those not of her family obviously couldn't say no to Gran either. "What happens if we can't lure Essence into a trap with one of the vials?"

"That depends on Dante." Gran glanced at him before returning her attention to Emily. "It might be that his demon needs a greater incentive than a single vial of blood."

"You want me to be the bait?"

Emily tightened her hand over his. "We wouldn't let you face him alone."

He drew his hand from hers. "But you want me to face him again."

Gran spoke before Emily could. "Why don't you have a rest before we make any plans? You could stay here or," a smile slowly formed, "you might want to stay with your family."

Emily nearly laughed. Gran certainly knew how to distract a person.

Dante rose from the table. "I can see them? Now? Are they okay?"

"They're worried for you. A visit will set their minds at ease," Gran said.

Dante's excitement faded. "What do I tell them? Am I meant to lie to them?"

"You tell them what you think is best," Gran said. "If you're planning on seeing them, I suggest you go now before either of you are too tired to drive."

"I can drive for you if you want," Carl said.

Emily hesitated. He'd have to find a way back if

he played chauffeur for them. She started to shake her head, ending up smothering a yawn with her hand instead.

Carl pushed away from the table, fishing her keys from his pocket. "I'm driving. The hospitals are busy enough without you pair adding to their long list of patients today."

Emily wanted to argue, but the tone of Carl's voice clearly told her it would be a waste of time. "Thanks."

"I'll meet you out the front." Carl strode from the kitchen.

"I've got to get Cricket." Dante gestured towards the back door before heading towards it.

Emily nodded then turned to Louise. "Uncle Leo said the family has been investigating Eternally Flawless Beauty Cream. I want to read all the information."

Louise glanced towards Gran before she nodded. "I'll email it to you."

"Thanks."

Dante walked back into the house, Cricket at his side. He looked at each of them.

Emily could almost hear him wondering what he'd missed. "You ready to go?" When he nodded, she gave Gran and Louise a hug before leading the way to the front door. She stopped and faced him before she opened it. "Wait here a minute."

"Why?"

She was disappointed by the suspicion she could hear in his voice. "What are you worried about?" She half smiled. "I mean, other than the obvious. Demons."

"I can't believe you're willing to help me. I'm nothing to you."

She tried to think of a way to explain it. Holding up one finger, she said, "Don't move." She dashed into the lounge room and took one of the spare copies of Demonology. Returning to the foyer, she found Dante in the exact place she'd left him. She held out the book. "My great great grandfather wrote this. Patrick Hunter."

Dante took the book from her and stared at the cover. "This is about demons?" He met her gaze. "Will it tell me all I need to know about surviving them?"

"Not everything. To learn everything about demons, you'd need a library." A half smile formed. "Luckily, we have one of those too." She gestured towards the book. "This will teach you the basics. Give you a fighting chance."

"Thank you." He returned her smile with a grin of his own. "Not just for the book."

Her gaze was fixed on his smile and it took a few seconds for his words to register. "Uhm." Her mind was blank. Looking away from him, she saw the front door. "We should go."

He put a hand on her shoulder when she went to open the door. "It makes you uncomfortable for me to thank you?"

She was tempted to let him think that. "No." She stepped away from him and after putting on her boots, opened the door, not daring to look at his expression to see how he'd taken her words. Heading for the vehicle, she heard a laugh behind her. A soft, surprised sound. She couldn't resist glancing over her shoulder and was in time to see his surprised expression replaced by an unfathomable one.

Dante hurried after her to fall in beside her, remaining silent, Cricket at his side. Reaching the vehicle a few seconds before her, he opened the front door and stepped back gesturing for her to enter.

She stared at him before nodding in thanks and getting in. She watched him through the window once he'd closed her door, remaining there a moment longer before he opened the back door and got in the vehicle, Cricket jumping in after him. It took a great deal of effort not to turn her head to look into the back seat. Demons were far easier to understand than humans. And that was saying something, since most demons were completely incomprehensible. When she'd buckled up, she closed her eyes, tilting her head back as the engine started.

She didn't realise she'd fallen asleep until they pulled up and Leo opened the door for her. She blinked several times, trying to gather her wits while Leo introduced himself to Dante. "Does Dante's family know he's here?"

Leo shook his head. "I thought it best to give him a few minutes to collect himself first. They're out the back." He looked past her. "Your sister has fallen in love with one of the horses."

"That sounds like Jane. She's pestered Mum for one ever since she was old enough to talk." Dante swung his door open and had to wait for Cricket to dash past him before he could get out, the book tightly held in one hand.

Emily smiled, getting out of the vehicle when Leo stepped back. She looked over to Carl. "Thank you."

Carl nodded, smiling in answer.

"Do you need a lift?" Leo asked. "I can get one of the boys to take you back to Gran's."

Carl got out and came around the vehicle, handing

the keys to Emily. "Mum will be here soon to pick me up. But thanks."

"Take care." Leo clapped Carl on the shoulder.

Emily bit back a smile when she saw Carl stagger slightly, always glad to see she wasn't the only one. "Where are Dante's family? Your backyard isn't exactly small."

"Saul is teaching the young one how to groom horses. Rainbow is sitting on the verandah and the older one is throwing rocks at the trees, glaring at them as if they're at fault for everything."

She couldn't help smiling at Leo's description. "I'll show him where they are." She reached for Dante's hand. "You ready?"

Dante nodded once, walking beside her as they went around the house rather than through it, Cricket beside them.

When he remained silent, she wondered if she should ask him if he was okay. Several glances towards him didn't help her figure it out.

"What's wrong?" Dante stopped walking, tugging her back to him when she would have kept moving.

A half smile momentarily appeared as she looked up at him. "Are you okay?"

"I don't know what to tell them."

"What would you normally say?"

"The truth."

"Then try that."

"What if they don't believe me?"

She shrugged. "Have they ever doubted you before?"

"No, but..." His voice trailed off. A wry smile formed. "I've never had to tell them demons existed."

She squeezed his hand. "I don't know your family, you do. You need to figure out what to tell them." She glanced at the corner of the house that wasn't far from them, Cricket moving closer to it as he checked out all the new smells. "You probably want to work it out soon because they're around that corner."

Dante stared at the corner, his hand tightening on hers. "How do I convince them?"

"I have no idea. I've never had to convince anyone before."

He dragged his gaze away from the corner of the house and stared down at her. "Not even a boyfriend?"

Her breath caught in her throat and all she could do was shake her head.

"Why not?"

She swallowed twice before she was able to speak. "Neither of the boyfriends I've had became important enough to be told the truth."

Dante continued to hold her gaze, stepping closer and letting go of her hand. He reached up to brush strands of her hair back from her face, tucking them behind her ear. "How important would someone need to be before you told them the truth?" His voice was soft.

She leaned forward to catch all his words. It took her a few seconds before she could answer. "Love."

His fingers continued along her hair until they were at the nape of her neck, threaded through the strands so his fingers made contact with her skin. He leaned closer. "Is–"

"Danny!"

He closed his eyes for a second, taking a deep breath before he let go and stepped back. Turning, he faced his sister who ran towards him, Cricket bounding along beside her. "Jane."

Emily drew in a shaky breath, almost glad he didn't sound thrilled by his sister's interruption.

Jane threw herself at her brother, asking a million questions all at once, not a single one of them making sense.

"Slow down." After returning her hug, Dante untangled her from him. "I'll tell you everything when we're all together."

Emily saw his mother before he noticed her. She

stood at the corner of the house, her hands pressed to her mouth, looking like she might pass out. Lightly touching Dante's arm, she nodded in his mother's direction when he looked at her.

The moment he saw his mother standing there, Dante strode towards her. When he reached her, he wrapped his arms around her. "I'm okay. You don't have to cry. I am okay."

Emily stared at them wistfully. What she wouldn't give to be able to hug her mother like that.

"Who are you?"

Chapter Eleven

Dragging her gaze from Dante and Rainbow, Emily met Jane's stare, holding out her hand. "Emily Hunter."

Jane recovered from her surprise at being offered a hand to shake and enthusiastically shook hands. "You got one of them marks too." She pointed to Emily's wrist.

"Yeah."

"What do they mean?"

"Depends on who you ask."

Jane's brown eyes narrowed. "That's what they said."

Laughter was surprised from her. It seemed like a talent of Dante and his family. "I'm sure you'll find out the answer soon enough." She gestured towards Dante. "Why don't we find your other brother so Dante can tell you everything that's happened?"

Jane stared suspiciously at her before nodding and joining her family. It didn't take them long to find Heathcliff and they sat at the table on the back verandah. Emily had suggested she leave them to it, but Dante had snagged her hand, drawing her to him, asking her to stay.

She ended up sitting beside him, listening as he talked about taking Cricket for a walk and being grabbed from behind and tossed in a van. When they'd let him out, he'd been stunned to see Essence. Emily noticed he didn't mention the cuts on his chest, only said they'd planned to sacrifice him as soon as they found a second victim.

Emily found herself talking about dreaming of him, avoiding mentioning the start of the dream, and helping him escape. When she spoke about shooting the demon with her bow, Heathcliff stared at her, his eyes round and his mouth slightly open. As if realising, he closed his mouth and tried to look unimpressed. He didn't quite manage. Emily suppressed a smile even though she was tempted to let it escape. She doubted Heathcliff would appreciate being laughed at.

"What happens now?" Rainbow asked when they'd finished telling her of their morning.

"We wait," Emily said.

"For what?" Rainbow demanded. "For that woman to find him again? To kill him?"

"No. We wait to see if Essence can be trapped." She kept her voice soft, ignoring the anger in Rainbow's words.

"That's not good enough. We should be doing something."

"Mum-" Dante began.

Emily placed a hand on his where it rested on the table. "It's okay. She cares." Her own parents had protected her as fiercely. She turned to Rainbow. "I will stand between him and any demons Susan sends."

"We should kill her then it wouldn't be a problem," Heathcliff said. "You reckon you can use a bow."

"I can use a bow, but I'd never deliberately take a life. We also don't know if there are others working with her."

"Then what are we meant to do?" Rainbow demanded.

Emily held her gaze for a moment. "Wait." When Rainbow started to speak again, she raised her hand. "I know you don't want to wait. I know you wish there was something you could do. But there isn't. Do you want to get Dante killed? We have to wait. We need to figure out what they're going to do so we can come up with the correct plan to beat them."

"He likes to be called Dan." There was a wobble to Rainbow's words.

Emily glanced at Dante, a half smile forming. "I know."

Dante placed his other hand on top of Emily's that still remained on his. "You can stop worrying, Mum. They know what they're doing. They even wrote a book about it." He glanced towards the book that was in front of his brother, who'd flicked through it earlier.

"They tried to tell me you were dead. The police kept telling me to prepare myself for the worst. I can't lose you." Rainbow looked around the table, her gaze stopping on each of her children. "I can't lose any of you." Her gaze rested on Emily. "Do you understand? It would kill me if one of them died."

Emily held Rainbow's gaze. "No, it wouldn't. You'd only wish it had." She drew her hand from between Dante's. "I'll let you talk." She walked away before she gave into the tears that made her throat ache. Behind her she heard running footsteps. She spun to see Dante chase after her.

He grasped hold of her hands. "Are you okay?"

She tilted her head slightly to the side. For once it didn't annoy her that someone had asked. "I think I am." Or if she wasn't, she was on her way there.

She lightly squeezed his hands. "You need time with your family." A smile half formed. "And I need to sleep. If you let my uncles know when you're ready for sleep they'll find a bed for you." She held his hands a moment longer before she let go and walked away. Before she stepped into the house, she looked back at him and found he stood there watching her. He grinned at her and nodded once before he turned and went back to his family. She was the one left standing, watching him before she forced herself to go inside.

She headed to her room and grabbed a change of clothes. Leaving the satchel in her bedroom, she headed for the bathroom. After a quick shower she collected her bow and arrows from her vehicle and put them under her bed, falling instantly asleep the moment she lay down.

She had no idea how long she slept before the usual dream began. She watched helplessly as her parents walked down the hallway. She begged them not to enter the room, but like always, they didn't hear.

"Emily?" Dante shook her shoulder.

She stared up at him, his face in shadows, his body outlined by the light from the hallway. She couldn't believe she'd slept so long it was now night.

"You were having a nightmare. You were telling someone not to open a door. Who was it?"

She sat up, swinging her legs to the floor. "My parents."

"What happened?" Dante sat beside her.

"They opened the door."

"What happened to them?"

She stared at her hands clasped tightly together, trying to think how to tell him. There was no nice way to put it. She looked towards him, the light from the hallway showing his concern. "Demons got them."

He drew back from her as if struck.

She reached for him, holding tightly to his hand. "I'm sorry."

"Aren't I meant to be the one who says that?"

A half smile momentarily escaped. "I won't let the demons get you. I promise."

"How can you promise something like that?"

Because she couldn't accept any other outcome. "I can. Don't you think I can protect you?"

"You're pretty good with a bow." He glanced around the room. "But I don't see any weapons if demons should arrive."

"You're looking in the wrong places. Not that it matters. Demons can't get in here. It's only humans you need to be worried about."

"Where should I be looking?"

"You could start with under my bed." She reached for the bedside light, turning it on when he pulled away from her to look under the bed.

"There's a bow and arrows under here." He knelt on the floor, looking up at her.

"In the wardrobe. Back right hand corner." She watched as he shifted her clothes to the side and took out a sword.

"Any more?"

"Of course."

He returned the sword to the wardrobe, laughing. "Of course?"

She rose from the bed. "I'm a hunter." She shrugged. "We always have plenty of weapons. Including ones you wouldn't think were weapons." Hunters always kept weapons nearby. Demons didn't care if a hunter had retired or quit, they came after them anyway. So like all other hunters who'd quit, she kept her weapons handy.

"Like what?"

She opened the drawers of her duchess and took out a vial of holy water, holding it up. "One of the things a demon fears most."

"Water?"

"No. Holy water." She lifted the cross she wore on

a leather cord, from under her shirt. "Even words can be weapons against demons if you use the right ones."

"Like what?"

She returned the holy water to the drawer and let the cross fall against her shirt. "Prayers." She crossed the room, stopping in front of him. "I've trained my entire life to fight demons. I know their weaknesses. And I know my parents were caught in a trap. I won't let that happen to us. We'll have other hunters watching our backs if necessary."

He took the step separating them. "Why?"

His voice was so quiet she almost didn't hear the word. "Does it matter?"

"Would you do this for anyone?"

She tilted her head slightly to the side, staring at him a moment before she answered. "No." The word was barely spoken when he crushed her to him, his mouth meeting hers. She reached for him, losing herself in the kiss far longer than she felt she should before drawing away from him. When he started to speak, she pressed a finger to his lips. "Shh."

He took hold of her hand so he could speak. "You don't know what I was going to say."

She was beginning to read some of his expressions easily. He'd looked guilty. "I don't want you to apologise."

"What do you want?"

Her gaze rested on his lips before she forced herself to focus on what was important. "I have research notes to read. Do you want to help me?"

He looked momentarily startled. "Is that your way of saying no to kissing you again?"

"If that was what I wanted, I'd say so." She turned towards the door, glancing over her shoulder. "Are you coming?" She barely managed not to return his grin.

He took her hand, walking beside her to the study. "Does that mean you want me to kiss you again?"

She slowly shook her head. "Can we focus on getting out of this alive first?"

"And then kisses?"

A grin escaped and she looked away as she tried to control it. "We'll see what happens."

He leaned in close, his breath brushing her cheek. "That sounded very much like a yes to me."

She glanced towards him. Maybe he was becoming as capable at reading her as she was of him. She stepped into the study and turned on the computer that sat on the desk, the keyboard pushed out of the way from when she'd been working at it. "We need to focus. Maybe there's something we'll notice that the others haven't. After all, we've got up close to her and her demons."

"A little too close."

She pulled a second chair over to the desk and sat down, moving the book out of the way, and the keyboard back into place. "Then let's see what we can figure out so that doesn't happen again." She put on her dark framed glasses.

Dante stared at her. "You wear glasses?"

"Only for close work."

He slowly shook his head. "I can't believe you wear glasses."

She glared at him. "Is there a problem with that?"

"No. It's nice to know you're human, with human problems. The way you faced down those demons and got us out of there I did wonder a few times."

"I'm human." Her words were soft. And far from perfect. She couldn't bring herself to voice that thought.

He took hold of her hand. "I'm glad."

Not knowing how to reply, she drew her hand from his. "Let's see what Aunt Louise sent." She logged into her email account and, remembering she owed her grandparents a phone call, she sent an email to say she'd call them in a few days time. She wasn't up to talking to them yet. She opened the email

Louise had sent, ignoring the messages from her friends. There weren't as many emails as there used to be.

They spent hours reading over all the files, even printing out some of them. Eventually Dante pushed away from the table. "This is a waste of time. The woman is crazy. Shallow and crazy. None of that is going to help us against her." He waved towards the computer.

Chapter Twelve

After removing her glasses and placing them on the desk Emily stretched, remaining in her chair. "Maybe something will click. It's a lot of information to take in all at once. Sometimes it takes a bit to process things and for them to fall into place."

"I think you need more sleep. Either that or you're desperate."

"I don't need more sleep. I'm not in the least bit tired."

"How about desperate?"

She couldn't argue that one. "If you're tired, you don't have to stay up and help me."

"I can't sleep. I was pacing the hallway when I heard you earlier."

Rising from the chair, she reached for him. "You need to sleep. You can't function without some sleep."

He held her tightly, his hand pressing her head against his shoulder. "There's no point. I barely get to sleep when a nightmare wakes me."

She knew about that. Had barely slept in the weeks after her parents had died. She held him a little longer before she drew away from him. "I'll sit with you. It's…" She glanced towards the time in the corner of the computer screen, words failing her when she saw the numbers.

"What's wrong?"

Dragging her gaze from the screen, she met his, concern in the dark depths of his eyes. She opened her mouth, but no words came out.

"Em?" He reached for her, drawing her close.

"It's two forty-five a.m." She closed her eyes at the pain in her voice.

"What does that mean?"

"It's when they died. It's the time that was on my alarm clock after I'd dreamt my parents' death." She thought of Gran dreaming of her brother's death when she was eleven-years-old. That was too young. Far too young. How had she coped? Opening her eyes, she stared at Dante. "The first premonition isn't really a premonition. There's no time to save them. The one after can be saved. You can be saved. We'll figure it out."

"I'm sorry you had to see that."

"Me too."

"But I'm glad you came for me."

"I thought I might have been going crazy."

"That's kind of how I've felt ever since I found out demons are real." A wry smile formed. "I don't think I'll ever feel sane again."

She ran her fingers along his jaw at the place where the blood had been earlier. "Do you want me to watch over you?"

"With your bow and arrows?"

"If you want."

"Are you sure demons can't get in here?"

"Positive. It's impossible for them to enter blessed land."

"But Susan could."

So could other humans, but it was probably best not to mention that. "Yeah, Susan could." He remained silent long enough she thought he might not speak.

"You could join me in the bed."

"With my bow and arrows?"

"Without them would be more comfortable."

She was far more tempted than she'd expected to be. "I'll watch over you. With my bow and arrows."

"Let me guess, not in the bed either."

Another smile escaped. At the rate she was going the ability to smile regularly might actually return one day. "I'll get my bow."

He walked with her, waiting by the door as she collected her bow and arrows. "You know you don't need to do this. I mean…" His voice trailed off and he made a vague gesture with his hand.

"It's okay." She looked towards the hallway. "Lead the way."

Once in the room he was sharing with his brother, she settled into the armchair that was in the corner, her bow and arrows across her lap. Even though she didn't mean to, she drifted off to sleep, coming awake at a noise, her bow and arrow trained on it.

Heathcliff's mouth dropped open and he stumbled backwards.

She pointed the arrow away from him, carefully reducing the tension on the string. "Sorry."

"I'd barely moved when you had that pointed at me. Would you have shot me?"

She shook her head. "Not without checking first."

Dante sat up in bed, rubbing at his eyes. "What's going on?"

"Your girlfriend tried to kill me."

"I'm tempted to let her. Couldn't you have got up quieter? I was having a good dream."

She wondered if he'd noticed what his brother had called her. "I probably still would have heard him."

Dante looked towards her, smiling. "You didn't need to sit there all night."

"I didn't. Most of the night had already gone."

The bedroom door swung open and Jane peered in. "About time you're awake." She noticed Emily. "What's she doing in here?"

"Being my bodyguard." Dante rose from bed, wearing only his jeans.

Jane gasped. "What happened to your chest?"

"Nothing." He grabbed the shirt off the end of his bed and pulled it on.

Jane came forward, trying to lift his shirt. "They cut you?"

He tried to push Jane's hands away, a halfhearted glare for Emily. "Not much of a bodyguard, are you?"

She remained in the armchair. "Did you survive the night?"

He stopped fighting against his sister and smiled at Emily. "Yeah, I did."

Heathcliff swore. "Mum's going to freak when she sees your chest."

Dante pulled his shirt down, stepping away from his sister. "She's not going to see it." He turned to Emily. "I'm starved. How about you?"

"Yeah." She rose from the chair. "Let me put my gear in my room then I'll meet you in the kitchen."

After breakfast, they returned to the study to go over all the information again. Late afternoon had Dante rising from his chair in frustration and Emily suggesting they take a walk. He agreed, spending most of his time checking over his shoulder.

"You're safe here. There are cameras and other security measures around the property." She held his hand as they walked along one of the riding tracks that meandered across the property, her bow and quiver of arrows at her back.

"Why?"

"I'm not quite sure what you're asking."

He stopped and faced her. "Why do you need all the security?"

"This is a retreat. The family members that end up here are usually needing to feel safe or are hiding out. Demon hunting isn't in the least bit safe."

"Then why do they let kids do it?"

"Because we're targets. Demons hate hunters and if they can't take out the adults, they'll take out the kids. We train our entire lives, even if we never actually hunt demons. Part of it is about protecting ourselves."

"You'll keep doing it? Even though your parents died hunting demons."

She hadn't thought she would. Not because her parents had died, but because she hadn't thought herself capable. "Yeah. Someone needs to make sure they don't take over the world and our family has been doing it for centuries." She smiled slightly. "I was born to hunt demons. I couldn't imagine my life any other way." When he started to speak, she interrupted. "I wouldn't want to imagine any other way of life." Not with how lost she'd felt when she'd quit being a hunter for fear she'd get a partner killed.

"Even though it could kill you?"

Her bow and an arrow were in her hands in seconds, the arrow piercing a leaf that had been drifting to the ground, impaling it in the knot of a nearby gum tree. She stared at the arrow that vibrated a moment longer, relieved she hadn't lost any of her skill. Turning to Dante, she smiled. "You were saying?"

He chuckled. "I've seen how fast demons can move. You aren't as quick as them."

"No, but I don't need to be. I only need to be smarter." She lowered her bow.

"Can you use all the other weapons hidden in your room?"

She nodded. She was best with a bow, but more than proficient with everything else.

"Was it hard to learn?"

"I don't know. I was learning how to use them before I was old enough to learn how to read and write. Children's versions of them."

"Did you ever resent your parents for making you learn?"

She didn't even have to think about it. "Never. I was serious when I said I was born to hunt demons." When he continued to stare at her, his expression unfathomable, she asked, "What?"

"I've never known that. Never felt like there was something I was born to do. You're lucky."

She stared back at him, her head on a slight angle as she thought about his words. She hadn't felt very lucky during the past six months. "I guess I am." She held out her hand, the one without the bow. "I'm hungry. Why don't we see what my uncles have made for dinner."

Smiling, he took her hand. "As long as you weren't planning on doing any more research afterwards."

"I was actually thinking I might teach you the basics of using a bow. There's a practice area out the back."

"Sounds good."

They remained silent on their way to the house, Jane meeting them at the front door. She was full of questions about where they'd been and what they'd been doing. Her non-stop chatter also prevented dinner from being silent and she invited herself along when they went outside to practice with bows, Heathcliff trailing behind them.

By the time they decided to call it a night, Emily was beginning to think she wasn't much of a teacher. After she showered, she returned to her room to find Dante pacing. She paused in the doorway.

He stopped when he saw her. "How long until demons can find me again?"

"Sunrise tomorrow will be the end of your second day."

"Which means what."

"They might be able to find you. Or you might have another two days. It isn't exact."

"What do we do?"

She shrugged. "I don't know. But we can't stay here, not if you want to keep your family safe."

"Of course I do." He hesitated. "Am I meant to be on the move for the rest of my life? Always running?"

"No. We'll take care of Essence and then you can return to your life."

"What if I don't want to return to it?" He crossed the room to stop in front of her where she remained in the doorway.

"What do you want to do instead?"

He shrugged. "Whatever I do is going to seem pretty ordinary after this."

She reached for his hand to link her fingers through his. "Maybe you were born to hunt demons too."

"How can I have been? You saw me with a bow tonight. Jane was better than me."

Her fingers tightened on his. "That can be taught." She pressed her other hand against his heart. "Some things can't be."

"Like what?"

"The way you look out for your family. You didn't hesitate. Leaving was the logical choice."

"Of course it is."

She slowly shook her head. "You'd be surprised at the amount of people who wouldn't think so."

"Since staying obviously isn't an option, what are the choices? How do we take care of Essence?"

"It might take you facing him. A vial of blood might not be enough to draw him out."

He held her gaze before he placed his hand over hers. The one that remained against his heart. "I trust you, Em."

Chapter Thirteen

Before Emily could reply, a noise in the hallway had her turning her head, tensing. It was Jane. She stepped back, removing her hand from his heart and drawing him into the hallway so he could see his sister.

"What's wrong?" Dante asked.

"Mum won't stop crying."

Dante turned to Emily. "I've got to go." His fingers momentarily tightened on hers.

She half smiled. "Of course."

He grinned, threading the fingers of his free hand through her hair at the nape of her neck to draw her close, his lips pressing against hers for a moment before he drew away. "I'll see you in the morning."

She watched as he followed Jane. When he glanced over his shoulder she couldn't resist returning his smile before she slipped inside her room, shutting the door behind her. She leaned against the door, closing her eyes. For once the action didn't bring with it rivers of blood. She remained there for nearly a minute, savouring the normality of it before heading to bed.

Sleep came quickly and the dream started as it always did, her parents walking down the hallway. It changed as suddenly as it had started. She was in her vehicle, Dante beside her. They were both dressed in black jeans and black long sleeved shirts. Fairly typical clothing for demon hunters. In the dream she glanced at the address on the GPS, memorising it. In the way of dreams, it reformed and she stood outside a building, her bow and quiver on her back and Dante at her side a quiver on his back and a bow in his hand. She only knew it was him because she recognised his eyes. Like her, he wore a black balaclava that left only his eyes uncovered.

"I trust you, Em."

Then he was gone. She looked around, seeing she was out the front of a building in an industrial area. The place was deserted. She took a single step forward and felt the world rush past her until she was peering into a large room from a high vantage point. Two girls were chained to a wall, Essence and Flawless standing in front of them. Flawless had his arms crossed over his chest and a smile of anticipation curving his lips.

Essence had one hand pressed against the shoulder of a girl who was sobbing, pushing her against the wall she stood in front of, his hand drawn back and his claws ready. She couldn't see his expression, but she guessed he probably had the same anticipatory look as Flawless.

Dante stepped out of the shadows, a bow trained on the demons. An arrow was drawn back, ready to be fired. "I'm going to kill you for everything you did to me." He didn't get a chance to release the arrow.

In a blur of movement Essence was across the room, his hand tearing the weapon from Dante and throwing it aside. "We have things to finish, but it won't be me who dies."

"Are you sure about that?" Dante threw holy water in the demon's face and he roared. Dante spun, running from the room.

Essence waved Flawless back. "Guard the sacrifices. The boy human is mine." He strode from the room.

The moment Essence left, Emily aimed her bow at Flawless. He raised his hand, a curved dagger glinting in the light. She released the arrow and it pierced his forearm, the dagger dropping to the ground as he spun to face her.

Emily woke, reaching for the bedside lamp as she sat up, trying to remember every detail of her dream. There was a knock on her door. She stared at it for a moment before speaking. "Yes?"

The door opened and Dante stood there. "I couldn't sleep." He gestured towards her lamp. "You couldn't either?"

She stared at him, not sure what to say.

He crossed the room. "What happened? A nightmare?" He sat beside her, taking her hand.

"It was a dream." She wasn't sure if you'd call it a bad one. Not since she didn't know how it ended. And it had been far better than her usual dream that always finished with copious amounts of blood.

"Want to tell me?"

Hesitating, she looked at the alarm clock. It was almost a relief to see it wasn't two forty-five a.m. It wasn't quite midnight. She froze, a certainty filling her. Those girls had little more than three hours to live. She faced Dante. "Do you want to be a hunter?"

"Will I survive the experience?"

"I don't know. I didn't see the end. All I saw were two girls about fourteen or fifteen-years-old, who were terrified it was their last minutes. One of them was pinned against the wall by Essence while Flawless watched the entertainment. They're replacements for us."

He reached out, running his hand down the side of her face. "I meant it, Em. I trust you." He held her gaze before he rose, tugging her to her feet with him. "Do I get a weapon?"

She grinned.

A smile slowly formed and he chuckled. "It's a bow, isn't it?"

"Yeah." She glanced towards the doorway. "We don't have long to get ready. They die at three."

He looked her up and down. "I'll leave you to dress. I don't think pyjamas are the right outfit to stage a rescue in."

"You're not scared?"

"Absolutely terrified."

"Good. I was recently told that any sensible person should be when it comes to demons." She took a step away from him. "Wear black. Blood is less noticeable on it."

"I hope that wasn't you trying to be reassuring."

"No."

"That's a relief. Because you certainly weren't." He strode from the room.

She closed the door behind him before dressing all in black. She collected her bow and arrows from under the bed, put her case of lock picks and several vials of holy water into the pockets of her jeans and grabbed a sheathed dagger. Picking up her satchel, she slipped her phone inside and took out the keys. Dante was waiting for her in the hallway and she gestured for him to follow. She headed for Leo's room and knocked on the door. It didn't take him long to open it.

"How can I help?"

That's what she loved about her family. "I need a bow and arrows for Dante. We have somewhere we need to be before three."

Leo swung his door fully open. "I'll come with you." As he spoke he gathered his bow and arrow filled quiver.

"We were alone in my dream. Both in my four-wheel-drive and in the building."

Leo handed over his weapon to Dante. "That doesn't mean you were alone. Or without help nearby. Give me the address. I'll get a handful of hunters together and we can stay back so no demon notices us."

"Okay. Thanks." She waited for him to get pen and paper and wrote it down for him. "We better go." She started to turn away. "Do you have balaclavas? We were wearing them in the dream." She guessed she better get used to calling it what it really was. "Premonition." She planned to have them for the rest of her life. Dante was going to live.

Leo strode to the chest of drawers on the wall across from the foot of his bed. He took two balaclavas out of the bottom drawer and gave them to her. "Is that everything?"

"I think so."

Leo clapped her on the back, causing her to stagger slightly. "Go with God." He turned to Dante. "You too."

With a nod, she strode towards the front door, Dante at her side. When they stopped on the front verandah to put on their boots, Cricket came over to them. Slipping the dagger down the side of her boot, she smiled when Dante patted Cricket's head and told him he needed to stay. She straightened. "Let's go."

"Will you tell me all the details on the way?"

Reaching her vehicle she nodded and got in the driver's seat, waiting until he was also in before she spoke. "It's not very sensible." Starting the vehicle, she headed for the highway.

"I've already done sensible for the morning. Let's talk about crazy."

A half smile tilted the corners of her mouth, almost turning into a full one. "It's certainly crazy enough."

She gathered her thoughts and started from the beginning. With her parents.

By the time they reached the address she'd remembered, from her premonition, they'd talked over all the possibilities, as well as spoken about the impossible, answered several phone calls from Leo and Gran and talked strategy. They sat in the dark, very little light from the nearby streetlights entering the vehicle. Both were silent as they pulled on balaclavas and reached for weapons.

Dante tucked the small vials of holy water Emily had given him into the pockets of his jeans. "I'm ready."

Emily turned her phone to silent and slid it in a pocket. She wasn't about to leave it behind this time. She'd have to be careful not to lose it when she fought the demons. "I don't suppose you've got a phone."

Dante shook his head. "I have no idea what happened to it when they grabbed me. I'll meet you back here if we get separated."

"Okay." She opened the door, having already made sure the overhead light was turned off. "Give me ten minutes to get in place first." She gave him the car keys. "Did you see where I got them from the night I rescued you?"

He nodded.

"Are you sure you're okay with this?"

He took his balaclava off, doing the same to her balaclava, pulling her to him, his lips meeting hers. When he drew away, he ran his fingers down the side of her face. "I trust you. Absolutely. Besides, I'm sure you'd dream where I was if you misplaced me."

"It doesn't work like that. There's no guarantees." She pulled her balaclava back on, wishing there was a guarantee.

"I know. But there's two girls in there who are needing one." He gestured towards the building.

She stared at his shadowy figure a moment longer before nodding. He was right. "Let's give them one." She got out of the vehicle, closing the door, one last look at Dante's shadowy figure before she strode to the building. Scanning the area, she tried to decide the best approach. No features stood out, shadows making it difficult to see most of the building. Circling it, she found a ladder leading up the side. It seemed a likely choice. Especially since she'd been looking down into the room in her premonition.

It took her longer than she'd expected to find the right location and far more willpower than she'd thought to remain hidden when she saw the two sobbing girls. She didn't dare check the time on her phone. The glimmer of light might catch the demons' attention. She could only guess it must be getting close to three. Dante better hurry up. She kept her bow trained on the demons. Flawless laughed when one of the girls screamed at something he said to her. For a moment Emily wished she was close enough to have heard, instantly changing her mind. She didn't want to be that close. Not to demons. Taking them out from a distance was the more sensible option.

Essence grabbed the other girl by the shoulder, drawing back his hand. She struggled to escape and he slammed her against the wall, causing her to scream.

Emily almost fired the arrow, fearing Dante would be too late. He entered the room and she breathed out slowly, trying to remain calm. This was her life. Her calling. They could do this, the two of them together.

Dante kept his arrow aimed at Essence. "Let them go."

Essence spun to face him, waving Flawless back. "What did you do to yourself, human? You smell different."

"I needed a transfusion. You were the one who took blood from me."

Emily was glad Dante had found a way not to lie. The demon would have heard it.

Essence scanned the room. "You've come alone? You think you can face us without help?"

"I'm going to kill you for everything you did to me."

Essence was a blur of movement, crossing the room to tear the bow and arrow from Dante's hands. He flung them from him. "I can hear the truth in your words, but that doesn't mean it will come true. You humans regularly delude yourselves."

"You think I can't kill you? Or send you back to hell?"

Emily held her breath, most of her attention trained on Flawless. If he even thought about moving, she'd shoot him.

"We have things to finish, but it won't be me who dies." Essence cackled. "No matter what you believe."

"Are you sure about that?" Dante tossed the uncapped vial of holy water in the demon's face. Essence roared and Dante spun, running from the room.

Chapter Fourteen

When Flawless started to move forward, Emily nearly fired the arrow.

Essence waved Flawless back. "Guard the sacrifices. The boy human is mine. Do not interfere. When I return we'll continue." He strode from the room.

Flawless grinned at the girls. "He didn't say anything about leaving all the fun until he gets back." He raised his hand, a curved dagger catching the light.

That was the signal she'd been waiting for. She took aim. Releasing the arrow she watched as it pierced his forearm, the dagger dropping to the ground. The two girls screamed as Flawless faced her direction. She had another arrow drawn and aimed at him, letting it go. He roared when it pierced his chest.

The girls screamed again, reaching for each other, the chains giving them enough length to clasp hands.

Emily had used all her arrows bar one by the time Flawless reached her. He'd lost his human shape to become spider like in appearance as he'd scurried up the wall to land on the narrow walkway that went the length of the room. She kept the arrow trained on him. "Return to hell. There's nothing here for you."

"There's power." He took a step towards her. "Unimaginable power."

She fired, aiming for his eye, slipping her head and arm through the bow so it was slung across her back.

Roaring, he ripped the arrow out, clawing at his face, blood running down his cheek, a red dark enough it might have been black.

"Return to hell. In God's name, return to the place you came from." She drew the dagger from her boot. It had been blessed and dipped in holy water. It wouldn't take much of a cut for him to feel it. She watched him, waiting for him to make a move, not even daring to glance towards the now silent girls to see if they were okay.

With another roar, the demon launched himself at her.

She struck out at him as she ducked, coming up behind him. A thin line dripped blood and she sliced him several more times before he backed away warily. She followed, beginning to pray out loud, determined to return him to hell so she could release the girls and find Dante. He didn't have an endless supply of holy water and she didn't want anything to happen to him. He was relying on her to rescue him.

Snarling, Flawless launched himself mindlessly at her and she slipped past him, sinking the dagger into his back, drawing it out before he could face her. She was again behind him when he turned. Over and over she attacked, always out of his reach, her praying slowing his movements as the holy water in his system burned.

With a roar that echoed throughout the building, he launched himself at her again, disappearing into dark smoke as her blade connected with him.

She stared at where he'd been, the burn in her wrist only an itch. Essence was still in the area. Dante better be okay. Running to the far end of the walkway, she clambered down a ladder. The girls remained silent. She wiped the blade on the leg of her jeans before putting it away.

"Who are you?" one of the girls asked.

She had no reply for them. She was still trying to figure out the complete answer to that question for herself. "Give me your hands." It didn't take her long to release them with the help of her lock picks. When one of the girls tried to throw herself at her, she held up a hand, stepping to the side. "You're not safe yet." She collected the dagger Flawless had dropped on the ground and the bow Dante had left behind. The arrow was broken. "Come on." She threw the words over her shoulder, looking for the exit. She ended up finding several dead ends before she found it.

The girls huddled together against the front of the building. "What do we do?"

She didn't have a clue. "Don't move." She stepped away from them before she rang Leo.

"How can I help?"

"I have two girls that want to be anywhere other than here."

"I'll send Aunt Louise and Carl. You call me if you need any more help."

"I will. They're at the front of the building."

"They're on their way. Tell the girls you've called doctors to tend to them. Not to be worried."

"Okay. Thanks." She disconnected, returning her phone to her pocket. "Two doctors will be here shortly."

"What about the police?" It was the same girl who'd asked all the other questions.

"They can't help you." A roar caught her attention.

It had sounded like Essence. "I have to help my friend. Don't move from here. They'll be with you shortly." She ran around the side of the building, heading for the back, which was where she'd heard the roar come from. She clutched hold of Leo's bow, wishing she had arrows to go with it. When she saw Essence slash at Dante, her heart plummeted, fear racing through her. "No!"

Essence turned in her direction, snarling before loping towards her.

"Em!"

Dropping the dagger she kept running forward, grabbing the arrow Dante had thrown to her, fitting it to her bow and shooting Essence. Another arrow arced through the air and she caught it, sending it into the demon's chest. If he'd had a heart she would have pierced it. She had no idea what internal organs demons had, but the arrow barely slowed him down. "Return home."

"This is my home, hunter. It has been for a century. You forget we once roamed this world without interference."

She watched him as she inched around him towards Dante. "Then you've been here too long and it's past time you returned to hell. Permanently."

Essence cackled. "You think you can do that?

Think you can force me to stay where I don't wish? My girl will call me back."

"She owns you?"

"Nice try, hunter. I own her. I've been at her side since she was a small child and called me back to her, playing at games she didn't understand. I've raised and guided her. Taught her to be what I want."

"What do you want with a human?"

"That is none of your concern. But you will assist me all the same." He leapt forward, slashing out at her.

She blocked him with the bow, dodging to the side, coming closer to Dante who held out several arrows. Taking one, she aimed it at Essence. "If you get sent to hell you'll lose all the power you've gained. I doubt that'll please you. Especially since you have so little after such a long time here."

"You know nothing. My power is already here and I will have it again." He leapt towards her again, his claws slashing at her.

She fired another arrow at him, nearly tripping over Dante when she dodged out of the way. With a scream of pain, Essence bounded away, disappearing into the night, the itch in her mark fading.

"Was that meant to happen?" Dante stared in the direction the demon had taken.

"It doesn't matter. The girls are safe. We're safe. That's all we needed to do here." She scanned the area. Demons weren't all to be wary of in a deserted area at night.

"How about this?" He held his left wrist out to her. "Was this meant to happen?"

She stared at the small mark that had formed at his pulse point, not even a centimetre long. For a second she felt like apologising to him. A half smile escaped and she met his gaze, repeating her earlier words. "Maybe you were born to hunt demons too."

He lowered his arm, stepping close to her. "Maybe." He tugged at his balaclava. "Do you think we can take these off now?"

"Let's get out of here first." She led the way when he nodded, picking up the dagger and an arrow, wishing there were more left. It would be okay though, she couldn't feel any demons in the area and she hadn't seen anything else to worry about. They were safe. For now.

"What are we going to do about Essence?"

"Someone has his power."

"How do you know?"

"He pretty much told us." She tilted her head to the side as she looked towards Dante. "We need to go over the research again. With this new information in mind."

He groaned.

She almost smiled at his reaction. "There has to be a reason he chose to stay with her for so long. And how would she have known about demons and how to call them? Now we have something to work with. We did more than save the lives of those two girls."

"I froze when I saw them. I nearly didn't step into the room."

"Why?"

"I knew one of them. Not well. We went to the same school last year. She was in year eight."

They reached her vehicle and she scanned the area before she fetched the key from underneath. The girls were gone. "A good thing we wore the balaclavas then." There was more light out the front of the building than had been out the back. She stared at the darker patch on Dante's shirt. "You're hurt." She tried to lift his shirt, but he prevented her.

"You're as bad as Jane."

She tried again, relieved to find only shallow cuts. "They'll need cleaning and bandaging. Did you lose much blood? Did he consume it?"

"Yeah. Why does it hurt like that when he does?"

She ignored his question, focusing on the

important part. "He'll be able to track you again now."

"I guess another transfusion isn't possible."

"No. Let's go. Before he decides to return with an army." Who knew how many demons Susan had control over. She put the dagger, bows and quivers on the back seat before getting in the vehicle. The moment Dante was seated beside her, buckled up, she drove away from the building. "Can you ring my uncle for me?" She handed over her phone. "We need to let him know what happened. And I want to find out if the girls are okay." The sun was starting to rise so they could stop worrying about major demons until it set. There was only Essence. And Susan. More than enough problems for now.

The phone barely rang once. "Are you safe, Emily?"

"We both are. How are the girls?"

"Aunt Louise said they'd be fine. They kept asking her if she knew you. She said you'd rang her for a house call." Leo chuckled. "One of the girls apparently kept telling her there was no house. And why would she go to a place with no house. Aunt Louise said she'd thought it was a work accident, but the girl could only focus on there being no house. Carl said she's suffering shock. But apart from that, she's fine. The other girl will probably hang on until they're in a safe place before she goes into shock."

"I'm glad. We're fine too, but Essence tasted Dante's blood again. We need somewhere to rest."

"Church? I can organise a few people to watch over you."

She glanced towards Dante, not sure if that would be a solution he'd be happy with. It didn't matter. He'd have to realise religions weren't always a contagious disease. The church was a public place that no demons could enter. They'd be safe from all demons there, including Essence. Hopefully Susan wouldn't want to start something around other people. She was too well known after appearing on all the ads for her beauty cream. "Okay, Uncle Leo. Has someone got a laptop I can borrow?" It'd be easier to read the information on a larger screen than her phone. "Or a tablet?" She was tempted to ask for her glasses too, but she'd manage.

"I'll see what I can organise." Leo paused. "How's my bow?"

She couldn't hold back the laughter that bubbled up. "I'm surprised it wasn't your first question."

"Well?"

"It's fine. More than fine. Ask Essence. He'll tell you it works very well."

Leo chuckled. "I'll collect it from you later. Drive carefully."

When the phone call was over, Dante asked, "Why a church? Couldn't we have gone somewhere else?"

"Demons can't enter them. They can enter some of the modern ones that haven't been blessed properly, but we're not going to one of them. We'll be safe there. I also doubt Susan will want to be caught doing anything illegal in a public place."

"Somewhere with a bed would have been better. I think I could actually sleep."

"There's nowhere safe that has a bed." She glanced towards him, trying to see how he'd taken her words. She wasn't about to lead Susan to Gran's house. "That will change. Eventually." They now had a clue. Hopefully it would help make sense of all the information she'd read earlier. There were a couple of things she wanted to check. Some articles she wanted to read again. It finally felt like they were making progress.

Chapter Fifteen

When they pulled up near the church, Emily found Leo waiting for her. He took the bow and quiver she gave him, giving her a tablet and two burgers. She put the tablet in her satchel. "Thanks."

"Sorry it's such an unappetising breakfast." Leo stared at Dante's shirt. "How injured are you?"

"A scratch," Dante said.

"I've got a first aid kit in my vehicle. We'll get you cleaned up and give you a fresh shirt before you go into the church. You'll draw less attention."

Leo ignored Dante's protests and his cuts were cleaned, dressed and he was given a black t-shirt. One that was a little too large for him. He ate the burger, Emily having already finished hers, while she talked possibilities with Leo. Before they headed to the church, she clasped Leo's left arm, their demon marks pressed together.

"Father Joe is out visiting a parishioner, but he'll be back after lunch."

With a nod, Emily let go of his arm and took hold of Dante's hand, continuing to hold Leo's gaze. "Thank you."

Leo clapped her on the back, causing her to stumble, before he got in his vehicle and drove off.

Emily watched him drive away before she turned and headed to the church. She dipped her fingers in the font, making the sign of the cross, shaking her head at Dante's questioning look. She led him to a pew at the back and knelt for a few minutes, offering a prayer of thanks before she sat and turned on the tablet, zooming in on the page to make it easier to read without her glasses. It didn't take her long to log into her email account and begin to go over the information again. She held the tablet so Dante could read it too. By mid morning she was struggling to remain awake, yawning as she brought up the next lot of information. She also had a headache from all the reading she'd done without her glasses.

She read the headline twice. 'Good Genetics May Play A Part In Susan Lunsford's Flawless Looks.' The pace of her heart picked up. This might be the information she was looking for. She tried to focus on the article, but it was difficult when all she wanted to do was sleep. She scrolled back to the start of the article.

"I haven't finished reading that," Dante said.

"I have no idea what I've read. I feel like I keep falling asleep."

"The short story is that her grandfather looks very young for his age. Competitors tried to claim it was genetics and not her miracle beauty cream and she said her grandfather was the first test subject, not her. He prefers to avoid all the fanfare as he's a private person."

She scrolled down a bit to stare at a photo. The caption underneath read 'Seventy-Eight-Year-Old Donald Lunsford'. The man wore a suit, had white hair that was neatly styled and his skin looked like it belonged to a man half his age. "I've got a feeling this is the one who stole Essence's power. And I bet he's also the one Susan learned how to summon a demon from. Either deliberately or accidentally." Even though she was excited by the discovery, it wasn't enough to keep her from yawning and her eyes wanting to close.

"How do we find out?"

A half smile made a momentary appearance. "You're not going to like the answer."

Dante groaned. "Research, isn't it?"

"Yeah. It starts with research." She yawned again, unable to keep her eyes open as she did so.

Dante put an arm around her shoulders and drew her close, taking the tablet from her hands and putting it on the pew beside them. "Rest first. Are you sure we can't go somewhere with a bed?"

She leaned against him, her answer little more than a murmur as she stopped trying to keep her eyes open. Sleep claimed her instantly and she dreamt. Actual dreams, not nightmares or premonitions.

A noise startled her from sleep and she found she was still leaning against Dante, his arm holding her near. She looked around, guessing it was the person in the process of sitting in a pew a couple of rows ahead of her that had disturbed her sleep. Checking the time on her phone, she discovered she'd slept for nearly five hours. They'd been surprisingly restful considering she'd been sitting up. She looked towards Dante who was rubbing his eyes, stretching. "You up for a bit more research now?" She reached past him and picked up the tablet, turning it on.

"I'm not so sure I was born to be a hunter if it involves all this research."

"It's not all about fighting." Although she guessed it was for some family members. But she'd always enjoyed research. Particularly when the puzzle pieces started to fit together.

"Do you think we can leave here long enough to get something to eat?"

About to answer, she found the information she'd been looking for. Donald's address. From the pictures it looked like he lived in what could only be called a mansion. It was set on a spacious block of land in a wealthy suburb. She stared at the time on the tablet. Surely they'd be able to check it out before the sun set. Who knew what major demons Susan would have searching for them once the day ended. She turned to Dante. "Drive-through be okay?"

"I'd eat almost anything right now."

Emily rose to her feet. "Let's go then." On the way to her vehicle, she sent a text message to Leo letting him know what they were doing. He sent one back telling her to be careful. She slipped the phone into her pocket before she got in the four-wheel-drive and put Donald's address in the GPS.

Dante gestured towards where she'd put her phone. "What's up?"

"I was letting Uncle Leo know where we're heading." She pulled out onto the street. "Are you up for some research that's a little more active?"

"Of course. What are we doing?"

"Looking for demon power."

"That doesn't sound safe."

She glanced towards him. "It's not. I've got a feeling Essence knows exactly where it is and he'll be there not long after us. He'll probably be keeping track of which direction you're in." She again glanced towards Dante when he remained silent. "Are you having second thoughts?"

He chuckled. "I believe I've lost count."

"You don't have to come."

He reached out and rested his hand against her thigh. "Someone recently told me they think I might have been born to be a hunter. I probably should check it out and see how accurate they were." He grinned at her.

Indicating, she turned off the road and into a drive-through, slowly driving towards the menu board. The warmth of his hand soaked into her skin. "You let me know if you change your mind."

"You can't get rid of me that easily."

Conversation halted as they ordered food and slowly crept forward to collect it. She waited until Dante had finished eating before she asked if he'd drive, so she could look at a few more things online while she ate.

It didn't take her long to learn Susan had been

raised by her grandfather from the age of four and to share the information with Dante. Both of Susan's parents had died in a tragic accident. She couldn't help feeling sorry for the vulnerable orphan who'd called Essence to her. She had no sympathy for the woman who'd killed to be eternally flawless. She was no longer an innocent child.

"We're nearly there."

Emily looked up from the tablet, staring out the window at the mansions they passed. She didn't need to check the address. She knew the moment they reached the house. "Park in front of the next one rather than in front of Donald's house." She got out as soon as the vehicle stopped and waited for Dante to join her on the concrete footpath, the grass edging it neatly trimmed.

He took her hand, walking beside her when she headed back the way they'd come from. "What's the plan?"

"Can you feel it? The burn in your demon mark?" Her steps slowed as they walked past Donald's place.

He nodded. "What's it from?"

"Demon. A powerful demon." No wonder Essence had hardly any power. Donald must've stolen nearly all of it. Demon power was a strange thing. Until a demon had all their own power they couldn't gain much new power. Essence would want revenge for that. Once he had his power back.

"I thought we were looking for stolen power, not a demon."

"It's pretty much the same thing." At least in the way a demon hunter could sense it. Her steps slowed even further as she saw Essence come around the corner, striding towards them. She tightened her free hand into a fist, wishing she held a bow. Obviously she wasn't dreaming because one didn't appear in her hand.

"Shouldn't we be running?"

"Maybe. But not yet. Let's see what happens." She doubted they'd be able to run fast enough. Hopefully it wouldn't come to that.

"Ahh, we're back to crazy, are we?"

"Looks like it." She kept walking, stopping when they were a couple of metres away from Essence. She didn't want to be close enough to a life stealing demon for him to be able to touch her. "How long has he had your power?"

"You can't get in there. I tried."

"Maybe you can't."

"The place is a fortress against humans and demons. Do you think I haven't sent men to get it back? Men who'd be too scared to steal it."

She wondered what had happened to the men. Probably nothing good. "What if I can get it back for you?"

Essence's eyes narrowed. "Why would you want to do that?"

"Because then I can send you to hell with your power and you won't have any if you try and return. It would take you ages to bring all that power over from hell." There were other things she could do too, but she wasn't about to tell him that. There'd been enough truth in her words without needing to spill all her secrets.

Essence cackled. "Can't you feel my power? No one could stop me or return me to hell once I had it."

"So you think." She tightened her grip on Dante's hand when he looked like he might speak. They had to be careful what they told Essence.

"You have no idea what you're saying, hunter. I was once one of the most powerful demons on earth and in hell. Before I was trapped by the trickery of a man using a child. He lied through her. One day he'll pay and I'll smile while he begs for mercy, enjoying every minute of it."

This time when she tightrened her grip on Dante's hand it wasn't to keep him quiet. At Essence's look, she wanted to take a step back. "I can feel the power. But I don't have to face you alone."

"Will you make a deal then?"

"I don't make deals with demons."

"Then what?"

"For as long as you leave us alone I'll work on getting your power back for you."

"And that is not a deal?"

"No. That is a fact." She held Essence's gaze, not looking away even though he made her feel uncomfortable. Actually, it was more than uncomfortable. It was probably closer to terrified. She'd faced more powerful demons than him before. She pushed away the thought that she'd never faced ones as strong as the power she could feel trapped in Donald's mansion. "I can't work on getting your power back if I'm busy dealing with you and Susan."

"That goes for both of us," Dante said.

Essence looked from one to the other before his gaze returned to Emily. "Two days. If you haven't managed by then, I doubt you ever will."

She tried to think of how to negotiate without making it sound like she was trying to make a deal. "Humans need sleep. Two days is nothing."

"Three. And not a day extra." Essence turned and walked away.

Emily stared after him, a shiver running through her at the thought of what might happen if she failed to get his power back. She should probably be more worried about what might happen if she managed to steal his power. Nothing good would come of either option and a feeling of dread settled over her.

Chapter Sixteen

"Did you make a deal with him?" Dante asked.

Emily shook her head. "He made one with me."

"Do you think that was a good idea?"

A slight smile formed. "Of course not. Nothing is a good idea when it comes to demons."

"What now?"

"I have no idea." Still holding his hand she turned and headed back to her vehicle, glad he was beside her. She had never done anything so insane in her entire life. A slight smile started to form. She was definitely more her father's daughter than her mother's.

"How are we meant to get into Donald's place? I'm guessing it's probably going to have state of the art security."

"Yeah." As they reached the vehicle, she stopped

and looked at him. "We won't be doing it alone. We'll get help. My family will help us."

"Your uncles don't seem like the type to break into homes and steal demon power."

"You haven't met all of my uncles." She released his hand. "Let's go. We need to visit some people I haven't seen in a while." She got in the four-wheel-drive, thinking about her other uncles. Her father's brothers. Lock picking hadn't been the only skill they'd helped her father teach her. Even though they knew nothing about demons, she knew they'd help her any way they could. Especially if they thought it might be something to do with those who'd killed their brother. Neither of them had been convinced it had been a random killing.

Both of them remained silent as she drove to a less wealthy suburb. Most of the houses were in good repair, the occasional one looking like it needed a coat of paint and someone who cared about gardening. She pulled up in front of one that was mowed, but untidy, a BMX leaning against the front steps.

Dante looked out the window when she turned off the engine. "Where are we?"

She stared past him for a moment, noticing lights

were on with how close they were to the end of the day. "My father's youngest brother lives here."

"He's got a kid?" Dante stared at the bike.

"Yeah, but he's with his mum weekdays. During school or school holidays." She reached for his hand. "Don't say anything about demons. None of Dad's family know. He always said it'd only get them killed and they'd end up in hell along with those they'd sent there." She half smiled at the memory.

"Then how can he help?"

"We need to get into Donald's house. Uncle Ian will be able to help us with that."

"What do we tell him?"

She put the tablet in her satchel and slung it over her head and arm. "You don't tell him anything. It would take too long to explain it all to you. Don't worry. I've got it all figured out." With what she hoped was a reassuring smile she opened the door, glad he didn't have Essence's ability to hear the truth in words.

"So in other words you're making it up as you go along."

A burst of laughter escaped and she glanced over her shoulder, watching him as he got out of the vehicle. Okay, maybe he didn't need Essence's ability. He seemed to be doing all right figuring it out himself. She joined him on the footpath. "I have a bit of a plan. Don't worry, I'll figure it out."

He took hold of her hand. "I wasn't worried. I trust you. Remember?"

She held his gaze a moment longer before she headed for the front door, keeping hold of his hand. Taking a deep breath, she knocked on the door. When no one answered, she knocked again. She was about to knock one more time when the door swung open. "Hello, Uncle Ian."

The man stared at her for at least half a minute, his mouth slightly open. Closing his mouth, he ran his fingers through short brown hair, blinking his hazel eyes several times before he was able to speak. "If you're expecting to join me for dinner, you should have called first. There's only enough for one."

After how many times she'd avoided conversations and turned down various invitations from all her family his reaction wasn't surprising. "I actually came over to invite you somewhere. Probably much later tonight than dinner time."

"Typical. I don't see you for months and it's only because you want something." The humour in his voice ruined the complaint. His gaze went to Dante. "Am I going to get an introduction?"

"Dan, Ian." She looked from one to the other, her

gaze returning to Ian. "Think we can come in?" The conversation was definitely not one she could have on the doorstep.

Ian stepped back, continuing to hold the door open, closing it once they were both inside. "This way." He led them to a kitchen, gesturing towards the table that was at one side of the room. "What's wrong?"

She almost asked him what wasn't. Instead she sat down and took out the tablet, bringing up the image of Donald's home. "I have to get inside this place. There's something I need."

With a low whistle, Ian joined Emily and Dante at the table. "Nice pad. You sure you didn't want to try for something with a bit of a challenge, like a bank?"

"Mum and Dad were investigating these people when they died."

Ian took the tablet from her. "How valuable an item?"

"Very."

"It'll probably have some pretty major security then."

"Yeah."

"It might be easier to get them to bring it out of the house than for you to get into it. Would it be the sort of thing they'd grab first in a fire?"

Emily slowly nodded. "Yeah. It'd be the first thing he'd grab no matter the emergency." She tried to ignore the uneasiness she felt about a house being deliberately set on fire. "What about the neighbours?"

"Whatever we did, we'd keep it contained." He pointed at some of the information. "This the address?"

Contained. She could probably live with that. The two girls who'd been chained, waiting for death, came to mind. She'd have to live with that. "Yeah. That's the address." She watched as he pulled up a map.

"This back street would be the best one to send him down. If we start with a minor explosion in that direction first and then have explosions going off in all the other directions he should go that way without thinking it's a trap." He stared at Emily for a moment. "What about the cops? Have you talked to them?"

"I've got nothing concrete to tell them."

"You want me to destroy this dude's house on a guess."

"Uhm… yeah. Kind of." Maybe she'd been wrong and he did need more details.

Ian held out the tablet to her, waiting until she took it before he spoke. "I'll get the gang together." He rose to his feet. "When do you want this done?"

"Tonight."

"Gatecrashing dinner would have been simpler."

"You were the one who suggested a challenge." She rose to her feet, Dante doing the same.

Ian chuckled. "I guess that'll teach me, won't it?" He looked to Dante. "How do you fit into all this?"

Emily spoke before Dante could. "He gave me the information."

"You trust him?" Ian asked her.

"Yes. With my life."

Ian held out his hand to Dante. "Thanks. Whoever killed my brother and his wife have been allowed to roam free far too long."

Dante took his hand. "We're not completely certain. But even if we aren't about that, there are other things he's responsible for."

"What kind of things?"

"Cult type things," Emily said.

Ian swore. "I knew it. With the way they'd been killed..." His words trailed off and he slowly shook his head. "Do you need me to help you get the item?"

"No. If you can get him to take it out of the house, I can get it." Hopefully before Essence could. "Can you call me when everything's ready? I've got a couple of other things to sort out."

"Will do." He walked with them to the front door,

wrapping his arms around Emily, hugging her tightly. "Don't be a stranger in future."

When she was in the vehicle, she looked past Dante to wave to Ian before she drove off. "Can you ring Uncle Leo for me? Put the phone on speaker." She held out her phone to him.

Dante took the phone and made the call. Leo answered instantly. "Did you find the demon's power?"

"We should have it tonight."

There was a few seconds of silence. "You don't plan to do anything crazy, do you?"

She almost laughed. She guessed it depended on how you defined crazy. Someone completely insane would probably find her plan perfectly normal. "I want to return the power to Essence in a way that'll weaken him."

There was silence again. "I'll think about it and get back to you."

"I'll need to deal with it immediately. I don't think I'm going to have a lot of time once I get my hands on his power. He's going to want it back." And he probably wouldn't care who got hurt in the process.

"How else can I help you?"

"I don't need any other help from you tonight, Leo. I have others helping me." She kept the details to herself. Leo wouldn't appreciate her blowing up someone's house to get at demon power. She was willing to do whatever it took to keep her and Dante alive. She'd made a promise. And she believed in keeping her promises.

"Who?"

"Uncle Ian."

This time there was nearly a minute of silence. "In that case I doubt I'd agree with the methods. You do know there are always consequences."

"Yes." She was willing to pay them. Essence couldn't be allowed to have his full power and Susan couldn't be allowed to keep getting away with having people killed for her beauty cream. Once again she thought of the girls her and Dante had rescued. Leo sighed heavily enough Emily could hear it over the phone. She was tempted to tell him it was okay, but she knew it wasn't. "Some choices have to be made." If she was lucky she'd live long enough to atone for any wrong she committed tonight.

"I'll ring you back as soon as I know what you can do about Essence's power."

"Thank you, Uncle Leo."

"I know you're hurting, but Melinda wouldn't like you to do something against your teachings."

Her mother had always been by the book. "I had two parents teach me."

"Darren always skated a little too close to the edge sometimes." Leo paused. "Be careful. Don't go throwing your life away trying to avenge theirs."

"I'm not looking for revenge." Maybe in the early days she'd thought about it, but not now. They wouldn't have appreciated it. "I'm doing what I was born to do. Tracking down demons who've harmed humans."

"I'll ring you as soon as I have some information for you."

The call ended and Dante handed the phone back to her. "What do we do while we wait?"

"Visit Gran. I need to raid the armoury."

"Your family have an actual armoury?"

She laughed softly. "No. Not exactly. It's more of a family joke, but there are a lot of weapons stored at Gran's place.

"You're not planning on arming me with another bow, are you?"

"Yep. And probably a sword and a few daggers too. This is war. You can never have too many weapons." Even if he didn't know how to use them, she'd feel better knowing he wasn't unarmed.

They remained silent until they stopped in front

of Gran's house, pulling up in the driveway that was empty of all other vehicles. She reached for his hand, threading her fingers between his. "I won't let him get you."

"I trust you, Em. No matter what happens."

She tightened her fingers on his before she let go and got out of the vehicle. The front door was locked and she had to use her key. She found Gran in her bedroom, at her desk writing. She rose from the desk once she saw who it was.

Chapter Seventeen

Emily hurried across the room and wrapped her arms around Gran. She wanted to stand there far longer, but there were plans to make. And demons to deal with. "Did Uncle Leo tell you?"

Gran patted her on the back before releasing her. "He's talking to Father Joe. Between them they should come up with a solution."

"I came to borrow some weapons."

"You know where they're kept."

With a nod, Emily started for the door.

"Emily."

Nearly out of the room, she turned to face Gran, Dante at her side.

"Sometimes the choice between right and wrong isn't always clear. Then you can only do your best. We all make mistakes. We're only human. God forgives. As does your family."

Her throat tightened and she strode back to Gran, wrapping her arms around her again. "I love you, Gran."

"And I you, child." Gran stepped back. "You have work to do. Know you'll be in my prayers tonight. I have dreamt of you."

"A premonition?"

Gran nodded. "There were flames and power. Enormous amounts of power. But I have every confidence in you. You're a Hunter."

Yes, she was a Hunter. With another nod, she turned and strode from the room, grabbing Dante's hand as she passed him. She could do this. Father Joe would work out a solution to make Essence's power difficult for him to use, Uncle Ian would destroy Donald's home and her and Dante would return Essence to hell. Simple. She nearly laughed. Yeah, as simple as learning to fly when you had no wings. A good thing she had help.

She stopped in the room where extra weapons were stored in cupboards and drawers, a few swords displayed on the walls. She thought about what they'd need. Vials of holy water were first on her list. She handed some to Dante.

"I can't believe this room. Your gran's place looks

like any other house from the street. No one would believe this existed."

She took down a sword from a display on the wall, picking up a belt and a sheath to slide it into. "She still trains sometimes. Gran mightn't be as fast as she once was, but I pity any demon who tries to take her on." She gathered a second sword, daggers, arrows and a bow for Dante. Lastly she took a gold cross, on a leather cord, from a drawer.

Dante shook his head. "I don't believe in that."

Emily half shrugged. "It doesn't matter. Demons do. Wear it. I want you to be safe." Or as safe as it was possible to be when taking on demons.

Dante took the cross from her. "And this will keep me safe?"

"No, but it will help. The cross has been blessed and dipped in holy water. Both painful to demons." She glanced around the room one more time, trying to decide if there was anything else she needed.

"I'll wear it for you."

Before she could comment, Emily's phone rang. The display read 'Uncle Leo'. "Yes?"

"Where are you?"

"Gran's."

"I'm ten minutes away. Wait for me."

"Okay." When he disconnected, she returned her

phone to her pocket, meeting Dante's gaze. "Uncle Leo will be here in ten. You hungry?"

"Yeah."

She led the way to the kitchen and made them sandwiches. They were still eating when Leo arrived. He held out a vial that was larger than the ones they normally used for holy water. Taking it, she stared at the cross sitting in liquid.

"Holy water. And a blessed cross. Tip it over his power. Father Joe said the power was likely to be stored in some kind of sealed box or urn. You'll have to be quick because the moment you open it, the power is going to want to return to its rightful owner."

She slipped the vial into her pocket along with the smaller vials. "Thank you."

"Go with God, Emily." Leo hugged her, patting her firmly on the back.

"I can do this, Uncle Leo."

He released her. "I know you can." He turned to Dante. "You take care too. Your family sends their love." He held out a phone he took from his pocket. "Rainbow said this was found where you'd been kidnapped."

"Thanks." Dante took the phone.

"I'll leave you to it." Leo took a step back. "You

have only to ring me if you want help. The family is on standby in case you should need them tonight."

She swallowed past the lump that rose in her throat. "Thank you."

With a single nod he left.

Emily stared after him for a moment before she turned to Dante. "What's your phone number? In case I can't dream up your location if I misplace you."

He chuckled, exchanging numbers with her before they finished their food. After they'd eaten, they retreated to the guest room at the front of the house. They rested while they waited for Ian to ring. Emily on the bed and Dante on the floor with one of the pillows. He'd shrugged philosophically when Emily had told him it was there or the lounge chair. There was no way he'd be allowed to sleep in a bed beside her in Gran's house.

Emily tried several times to pick the ringing phone up off the bed where she'd left it lying beside her. "Yes?"

"Everything is set up. How long do you need?"

Sleepiness faded at the sound of Ian's voice. "I'm on my way. I'll give you a five minute warning call."

"Make that ten," Ian said.

"Okay." She rose from the bed, gathering weapons, nodding to Dante when he did the same.

"And Lee said to tell you that you better answer our calls in future or this is the last favour we do for you."

Emily half smiled, knowing it was an empty threat and neither of her uncles would fail her. "I will."

"And you need to come round for dinner one night. When the terror is here."

That was what he always called his son. It would be good to catch up with her cousin. "Okay."

"Good. I'll wait for you to call." He disconnected.

Slipping her phone into her pocket she stared at Dante, trying to figure out how she felt. A smile tugged at the corners of her mouth as she figured it out. Excited. She was more than ready to take on Essence. "Are you ready?"

"Yeah, I am." He sounded surprised. "I didn't think I would be."

"Hunter?"

He grinned, reaching for her and tugging her close. "Maybe."

His lips met hers and she clung to him, returning his kiss. When she pulled away, he grinned at her again and she saw excitement in his eyes. "Yeah, I'd say that's a little more than maybe." She tangled her fingers with his. "Let's do this."

They headed for the front door, with their weapons, locking it behind them. Emily's vehicle was the only one in the driveway. As soon as they were both in, their weapons on the back seat, she put the destination in the GPS and started the engine. A rush of excitement filled her. She'd missed this. Missed going on hunts and taking on creatures more powerful than her, forcing them to leave her world. Fighting with others to keep humanity safe. She wished her parents were here to help her. Neither spoke until they were nearly there.

"Are you scared?"

She glanced towards Dante, fearing he was going to change his mind. "Terrified."

"I can't believe we're doing this. When you feel terror you're meant to run in the opposite direction. Not to it. We're obviously insane."

"Or more sane than the rest?"

"How do you figure that?"

"Those that run are often caught. At least if we're caught, we'll go down fighting."

He slowly nodded. "I like that. Go down fighting. I can live with that."

Seeing the GPS said they'd arrive in ten minutes, she handed her phone to Dante. "Can you call Uncle Ian and put it on speaker?"

Ian answered immediately. "Ten minutes?"

"Yeah."

"Are you absolutely certain you want to go ahead with this?"

"Yes."

"Even though there could be innocent casualties?"

Why hadn't she thought of that earlier? She didn't want anyone to get hurt. "How likely is that?"

"Extremely slim. We did some checking. No offence to you, but we don't know Dan."

She nearly told Ian that Dante could hear him, but she doubted it would make a difference in what he said. "What did you find out?"

"A lot of rumours, nothing concrete. He's not a man to mess with. You sure you know what you're doing? I know your parents thought you were capable of all sorts of things, but well… they're not around anymore."

She doubted he'd led a quiet life at her age from what she'd figured out over the years. "What were you capable of at seventeen, Uncle Ian?"

Ian chuckled. "Fair enough." He paused a moment. "You there yet?"

"Pretty much."

"Enjoy the show. You'll have a front row seat." Again Ian paused for a moment. "Let me know when you're safe."

"I will, but it might take a bit. I'll be busy for a while."

"I'll be waiting to hear from you." Ian hung up and an explosion sounded.

Parking on the side of the street, Emily left the engine running and turned off the lights. Taking her phone from Dante, she slid it into her pocket. More explosions sounded and she saw fire through the trees. This had to work. Donald had to take the demon power out of there. She waited. The power didn't seem to be moving.

"What if it's in some kind of protective vault?"

"Then we'll have to figure something else out." Although she had no idea what they could do if this didn't work.

They remained silent, sitting together in the dark as they waited to see what would happen. In the distance there was the sound of sirens and yet the demon power remained in place.

"Should we stay here? What if the cops start searching the area?"

She checked the time on her phone. "We'll give him five minutes." She watched as the numbers slowly changed. When the five minutes were up, her heart plummeted. "Maybe another five?" She'd been so certain this would work. Hadn't Gran dreamt about flames? Although she guessed Gran hadn't dreamt they'd be successful.

Dante reached out and clasped her hand. "We've still got time. Essence gave us three days. We can come up with another plan."

She started to speak when she noticed the demon power coming closer. "He's moving it." She returned her phone to her pocket, relief and excitement rushing through her.

"What?"

"Donald. He's coming this way. Or at least someone is, with the demon power, and I doubt he'd let anyone else get their hands on it." Surely it had to be Essence's power. No other strong power would have been able to come into the area without her noticing. She stared along the street, trying to see if there were any oncoming vehicles. It remained empty.

"I don't-" Dante broke off, his hand tightening on hers. "They've got the headlights off." He pointed with his free hand. "Look."

Letting go of his hand she turned on her own headlights and drove out onto the street, blocking a fair portion of it as she did a three-point turn excruciatingly slow. The lights of the vehicle came on and they hit their horn, driving around her when she stopped in the middle of the street. She could sense the power in the car. It made her demon mark burn and fear rise.

Chapter Eighteen

Before the other vehicle had driven far Emily was beside her vehicle with a bow and arrow in her hands, shooting the tyre. The vehicle swerved, but kept going. Returning the bow to the back seat, she got behind the wheel again and took off after the other vehicle. She'd hoped that would have stopped them. At least it seemed to have slowed them down. Even if it hadn't, they wouldn't have been able to lose her. She could easily keep track of the demon power. But that meant others would be able to as well. She hadn't thought about that when she'd been making her plans.

"I always thought car chases were something from the movies until I met you. That they never actually happened in real life."

She gained on the car in front. "Don't get too used to them. They don't happen that often."

"You could have fooled me."

Her laugh was broken off mid sound as she tried to avoid a car coming from her right. It didn't take long to figure out it was after the demon power too. She couldn't tell for certain, but she guessed it was Essence. The second car crashed into the first one, slamming it into a tree. Seeing Essence get out of the car, Emily sped up, aiming for him.

"What are you doing?" Dante grabbed the handle above his window.

"Don't get out and keep a vial of holy water ready." She winced as she hit Essence, slamming on the brakes. The moment her vehicle stopped, she threw open the door and ran towards Essence who was lying on the ground. Grabbing a vial of holy water from her pocket, she threw it at the demon who struggled to rise to his feet.

He roared, clawing at his face.

Emily didn't pause to see what he'd do. She raced to Donald's car and wrenched open the back door. The old man was crumpled in his seat, the tree having hit near where he sat. She had no idea if he was okay and didn't have time to check. Grabbing the gold trimmed timber box from the seat beside him, she raced for her vehicle. "Here." She shoved the box at Dante, driving off before she'd had a chance to shut her door. A glance in the rear view mirror showed Essence on his feet, striding in her direction.

"What do we do now?"

She opened her mouth to speak, but never had the chance. A parked car flew out in front of her and she slammed into it, the airbags going off. She heard Dante shout, as if from a distance. There was a ringing in her ears and she tried to focus. The world seemed to recede. Dante appeared to be speaking, or at least his mouth was moving, and something damp trickled down the side of her face. Touching her fingers to it, she saw it was blood.

She wiped her fingers on her shirt. "Don't let him get my blood. Or his power." Sounds started to come back and the pain in her head made her feel slightly ill, a headache already starting.

Her door was wrenched open and she turned to see Essence staring at her, his feline face grinning, his claws held menacingly. "Give me my power."

Before Emily could say no, she felt his power rush past her, the demon roaring as it returned to him. Turning her head, she met Dante's gaze. "What have you done?" The cross in the vial of holy water was in her pocket.

He held up the cord that had once held the cross she'd given him. "Kept him from killing you."

"What have you done?" Essence snapped Emily's seat belt and dragged her from the vehicle. "What did you do to my power?"

The force of his power made her demon mark burn and her heart race. She tried to remain calm. "I didn't do anything." And it was the truth. She hadn't been the one.

"We made no deal. I owe you nothing." He kept hold of her.

She slipped her hand into her pocket. "I never make deals with demons." She tossed holy water into his face, pulling away from him when he loosened his grip. "Dante. Run." She opened the back door of the vehicle, grabbing weapons before she followed her own instruction. She handed the swords and a bow to Dante, keeping hold of her own bow and slipping the quiver into place. Drawing out an arrow, she came to a stop and spun to face Essence, firing several at him. Dante remained at her side. There was no way they'd be able to outrun Essence, but hopefully she could keep him away long enough. "My phone is in my pocket. Call Uncle Leo."

Dante retrieved her phone, putting it on speaker mode.

Emily continued to shoot arrows at Essence who slowly came closer. He didn't look happy. They couldn't beat him. Not with how much power radiated from him.

"Help is coming. We've been tracking your location with your phone," Leo said.

"Thank you." Her arrows weren't going to last much longer.

A car raced towards them, a dark all wheel drive. It pulled up, the front driver's side window lowering to show a young man with sandy blond hair, warm brown eyes and a silver cross-shaped stud in one ear. "Time to get out of here."

"Riley." Emily was surprised to see him. He was one of the family members she called a cousin and he was three years older than her.

"Come on, sweetheart." Riley grinned. "That demon doesn't look happy."

Dante opened the back door and got in the car as Emily fired her last two arrows at Essence before hopping in the back too. She'd barely closed the door before Riley took off. "Where are we going?"

"Sanctuary."

She rubbed at her forehead, trying to wipe away the blood. "A church? Looking like this?"

"I'll drop you at the front door. Father Joe will clean you up."

She didn't know what to say. The vial Father Joe

had given her was in her pocket and Essence had his power. Who knew if the blessed cross that had been dipped in holy water would be enough. She ran a hand over her face, wishing her head would stop aching.

Dante took hold of her hand, squeezing it lightly. "We'll figure it out." His voice was soft.

She looked at him, trying to see his expression from the light that flickered in and out of the car from passing streetlights. "Yeah." Somehow. She didn't know how yet. Checking the time, she nearly groaned. Two forty-five in the morning. She was sick of seeing that time.

When Riley pulled up at the front of the church where they'd spent most of yesterday in, he turned to them with a grin. "Nice explosions. I don't think many of the family will agree though. Attention is something we usually try and avoid around here."

She smiled weakly. "Thanks for the lift."

"Anytime, sweetheart." Riley glanced out the window. "You better move. I can feel him coming closer. I'd rather not be around when he arrives. Being stuck here until sunrise isn't exactly on my list of things to do."

Reluctantly leaving the weapons behind, Emily and Dante got out of the car and headed inside the church. Dante chuckled when she stopped to dip her fingers in the font. Once she'd made the sign of the cross she looked at him with a question in her eyes.

He shook his head slightly. "A house blew up, we've been in a car chase, was attacked by a demon and rescued by another hunter and yet you still stop to do that." He gestured towards the font.

"It's automatic." She glanced towards the altar where she could see someone coming towards her. She relaxed when she saw it was Father Joe. "In a way it's also what keeps the demons from entering here."

Father Joe reached them before Dante could say anything else. He looked from one to the other before holding his hand out to Dante. "I'm Father Joe. I guess you must be Dan."

Dante shook his hand, nodding.

Father Joe peered at Emily's head. "How about we get you cleaned up? Did you leave any blood behind?"

"I don't think so."

"Why does that matter?" Dante asked.

"Did you read the book I gave you?"

"No. I haven't had time. Between research and car chases I've been pretty busy."

She couldn't argue with that.

"I'll be back in a minute with the first aid kit."

Father Joe gestured towards the pews. "Take a seat. I won't be long."

Nodding, Emily turned to Dante when Father Joe walked away. He was staring at his wrist. "What's wrong?"

He held out his hand. The demon mark now went completely around his wrist. "Is it normal for it to grow this fast?"

She nearly said no, but the worry in his eyes stopped her. "That demon power you were playing with in the vehicle was pretty powerful."

"So I'm guessing that's a no."

There was nothing she could say, only nod.

"All right, let's go sit down." He grinned, one that looked a little forced. "Before my legs give out on me."

She slipped an arm around his waist. "Let me help you."

As they walked towards the pew, he put his arm around her waist. "If I'd known this would be the result, I would have said something sooner."

She laughed softly, sitting beside him. Meeting his gaze, she sobered. "I'm sorry. I thought we'd get him tonight." She barely managed not to rub her wrist that burned with how close Essence was. She bet that if she looked outside, she'd see him.

"You'll figure something out. Then we'll try again."

She nodded even though she wasn't certain he was right. "I better ring Uncle Ian and let him know I'm okay." She drew away from him so she could take out her phone and make the call. She put it on speaker so Dante could hear what was said too.

"Are you okay? Did it help?" The phone was muffled, but she could still make out Ian's words. "She rang me, Lee, not you."

She smiled slightly as she listened to her uncles. "I'm okay. It didn't help as much as I'd hoped, but we're one step closer." She had to believe that. She'd wanted Essence to have his power back. Well, he did. It was just far stronger than she'd hoped. "Were there any innocent casualties?" She held her breath, waiting for the answer.

"No. You can stop worrying about it. There was also no damage to any of the neighbouring properties."

"Thanks for helping." She paused. "Both of you."

"Anytime. You'll let us know as soon as you find out anything for definite about who killed Darren and Melinda?"

"Yeah." She saw Father Joe heading back towards her. "I have to go."

"All right. And Lee said to tell you that you've got to have dinner at his place too."

"Why don't we all have dinner together when I finish sorting this out?"

"It's a plan."

Disconnecting the call, she slid her phone back into her pocket and let Father Joe clean up the blood on her face. She was relieved when he told her it was superficial. A pity her headache wasn't as minor. A good sleep would probably help, but she had no idea when she'd have time for that.

Once he'd checked Dante over and put everything back in the first aid kit, Father Joe stood up. "Is there anything else you need?"

She wanted her bow and quiver full of arrows. "No. I'm fine for now." She turned to Dante who shook his head.

"Call me if you need me. I've let the other priests know you'll be in here till morning." He smiled. "Keeping vigil."

She nodded, a half smile forming. She'd used that excuse before. "Thank you."

Father Joe strode back towards the altar, heading through a door that was barely visible in the shadows.

"Now what?"

She had no idea. Rubbing her wrist, she couldn't

resist looking towards the exit. "We plan our next move."

"That's him making my mark burn, isn't it?"

"Yeah." She tried to think what to do. Tried to come up with a plan. Instead, she fell asleep and her nightmare started.

Chapter Nineteen

As Emily's father reached out to open the door, he reformed and she stood in front of Essence on the doorstep of the church as dawn approached.

"You can't hide in there forever." Essence cackled. "And if you think you can, I will soon send humans after you to prove that even in sanctuary you aren't safe from me."

"Killing Donald won't satisfy you."

"I don't plan to kill him. I'm going to make him suffer for decades. He'll wish for death, but I won't give it to him."

"It won't work. You try torturing him and he's likely to have a heart attack and die."

"You have a better idea? And if you do, why would you share it with me? You're my enemy."

"Who killed my parents?"

A look crossed Essence's face. One that had a touch

of victory in it. "The enemy of my enemy is my friend."

Emily woke, the words ringing in her head. She reached for Dante, shaking him awake. "I know what to do."

"A premonition?"

"Yeah." She checked the time. There wasn't much left until sunrise. Essence wouldn't be able to walk the earth during the day. Not with the power he now had. "Come on. Let's go talk to him before he's chased away by the sun." She slid a hand into his, holding on tightly.

"What are we going to do?"

"I think he's about to become our ally." She took a deep breath trying to steady the race of her heartbeat. "Temporarily."

"Ahh, another one of those crazy moments."

She laughed softly. "Yeah, one of them."

"You know the scariest part?" He walked beside her to the exit.

"What?"

"They're starting to seem not so crazy."

"When they no longer seem crazy, that's when you're a hunter."

"I'll let you know if that happens." He fell silent as they reached the front door.

Emily let go of his hand to open the door. It didn't take long for Essence to stride up to them, forced to remain outside of sanctuary.

"You can't hide in there forever." Essence cackled. "And if you think you can, I will soon send humans after you to prove that even in sanctuary you aren't safe from me."

A sense of déjà vu washed over her. The words from her dream came to mind. "Killing Donald won't satisfy you."

"Did you really think that was all I meant to do to him?"

"Plans don't always go the way you want them to." Last night was a perfect example of that.

"I don't plan to kill him. I'm going to make him suffer for decades. He'll wish for death, but I won't give it to him."

It felt odd standing there, speaking words to him that she'd already spoken. "It won't work. You try torturing him and he's likely to have a heart attack and die."

Essence stared at her for a moment. "You have a better idea? And if you do, why would you share it with me? You're my enemy. You tried to destroy my power."

"No, that wasn't what I was trying to do.

Remember, my plan has always been to send you back to hell. You arrived a little too soon."

Essence cackled. "Plans do fail." His eyes narrowed. "But a hunter doesn't befriend a demon."

She could have told him that wasn't always true, but she didn't have time. She could feel sunrise coming closer. She had to convince Essence before he had to leave for the day. "Who killed my parents?" It was a question she'd wanted answered so many times.

A look crossed Essence's face. One that had a touch of victory in it. "The enemy of my enemy is my friend."

It was almost an answer, but she wanted to hear the words. "Who killed my parents?"

"Those who own Eternally Flawless Beauty Cream."

Why couldn't he answer her straight? She nearly said those exact words, but Dante reaching for her hand reminded her to be sensible. "I need names. Who owns it?"

"Donald and Susan Lunsford."

She nearly closed her eyes at hearing an answer. Instead she steadily held Essence's gaze. "It would have to be both. You want Donald punished, Susan needs to be punished too."

"Are you making a deal with me?"

"I don't make deals with demons."

"It sounds very much like you're trying to make a deal with me."

"No. When they're out of the way, then you and I can finish up." She pointed at him. "I still plan to send you back to hell."

Essence cackled, throwing back his head, the sound seeming to go on endlessly. "How did that plan work out last time?"

"Plans fail. It happens. The next one won't."

"You may believe that, but it doesn't make it true."

Before she could argue with him, the sun rose and he vanished.

Dante stared at where Essence had been. "Was that meant to happen?"

"Yeah. But he'll be back. When the sun sets."

"And then what?"

She looked at him, continuing to hold his hand. "We pray our next plan doesn't fail."

"What about if I don't know how to pray?"

She glanced towards the colour staining the sky. "I have time to teach you before sunset."

"Maybe you should be teaching me to use a bow instead."

A half smile formed and she tilted her head slightly

as she looked at him. "Why? You starting to think crazy is normal?"

He chuckled. "Getting there."

Letting go of his hand, she slid her arm around his waist, leaning against him as she watched colour and light fill the sky. "I'll call someone to give us a lift to Gran's. We can rest there and figure out what we're going to do."

He wrapped his arm around her shoulders, holding her close. "We'll figure it out. Together."

That sounded like a plan to her. She continued to lean against him, not wanting to move. Eventually she had to, ringing Leo to ask for a lift. When he dropped her and Dante at Gran's, he told her he'd had her vehicle towed and it was being repaired. He also said Riley had put the weapons, she'd left in his car, in Gran's front lounge room. Thanking him, she headed for the lounge room, picking up her bow to run her hands over it.

Dante followed her into the lounge room. "It means a lot to you, doesn't it?"

"Yeah. It was the first weapon my parents ever gave me. One that was completely mine, not handed down or borrowed from someone else." She looked past him to see Gran stood in the doorway. "Essence got his power back."

Dante spun to face the doorway, taking a step closer to Emily as he did.

"Wasn't that your plan, child?" Gran came further into the room.

Emily shrugged one shoulder. "Kind of. We didn't get to use the holy water and cross on it first. He sent a car in front of mine." She glanced towards Dante. "But Dante did use the cross I gave him and Essence noticed there was something wrong with his power. How much of a difference it made, I don't know."

Gran nodded, her gaze on Dante. "Quick thinking."

"Em told me it was blessed and dipped in holy water. It seemed similar to what had been done to the other cross." He paused. "I dropped it into the box as soon as I opened it. It didn't seem like there was anything inside. I mean, it felt like something rushed out, but there wasn't anything there."

Gran slowly nodded. "That's as it should have been."

"Gran, I had another dream. A premonition."

"Why don't we all sit down, child?"

Emily waited until they were seated before she told Gran about her premonition and her talk with Essence. When Gran remained quiet, once she'd finished, she couldn't help worrying that she'd done something wrong. "Shouldn't I have talked to him?"

"It isn't a requirement that you follow the information given to you in premonitions," Gran said.

"Does that mean I shouldn't have talked to him?"

"It means you always have a choice. You must decide each time what to do with the information given to you."

"Then what are they for?"

"They're the best chance of success, not a guarantee of it though."

She wanted a guarantee. How else was she going to defeat Essence? She glanced at Dante, who was sitting next to her, reaching for his hand. If she didn't manage to defeat Essence, he'd destroy both of them. She'd done more than enough to annoy him and Dante had escaped. Both of them would have made Essence feel powerless and a demon didn't like that. "Do you think using Essence to bring down Susan and Donald will work?"

"Are you willing to use yourselves as the bait?"

She hesitated, not speaking until Dante squeezed her hand reassuringly. "Yes. What do you suggest, Gran?"

"A demon will go after anyone who has wronged

him. No matter how slightly. It is a necessity for them so they can maintain their power."

Emily nodded, wondering what Gran was getting at.

"If he was unable to take his revenge on you he'd be forced to find others who could do it for him. Others that could be trapped by not only the laws of demons, but also human ones."

"How would I do that? And what would make him help set them up when he can hear the lies in my voice?"

"Because you would tell him the truth. He'd be the one doing the lying, when he entraps the other two. Are you interested?"

She nodded and listened to Gran's suggestions, wishing the day wasn't disappearing so quickly. Night was likely to arrive well before she was ready for it. When Gran finished speaking, she nodded. "We'll try it." She had no other plan and her premonition hadn't given her enough details to know what had the greatest chance of success. She didn't want to die or let anything happen to Dante.

Gran rose to her feet. "Then you'd best get some sleep. It'll be a long night. I'll let everyone else know to be ready in case Essence does his part." She paused, looking from one to the other. "You will stay in the front guest room, Dante. And you will stay in one of the other guest rooms, Emily."

She couldn't resist smiling at Gran's words. Rising from the chair, tugging Dante with her, she nodded. She started to follow Gran from the room, but Dante pulled her back to him. Before she could ask what was wrong, he wrapped his arms around her, his lips meeting hers.

When he eventually drew away, Dante smiled. "We will beat him, Em."

"How can you be so certain?"

"Because I doubt you'd accept any other outcome."

She laughed. "Neither would you."

He reached for her hand, momentarily holding it. "Exactly. Which means we'll live. Both of us." He glanced past her. "You better go before your gran comes back here looking for you."

Gran wouldn't, but she nodded and strode from the room anyway. She found Gran in one of the guest bedrooms, waiting for her. She remained silent, wondering what Gran needed to tell her.

"I like your Dante. He has the heart of a hunter."

She wasn't sure how to reply to that so she nodded instead. From Gran that was a high compliment.

"The first one I saved, I ended up marrying."

Emily stared at Gran, open-mouthed. And she'd

thought she'd had no idea how to comment on the first statement. Marriage? She hadn't even had a long-term boyfriend.

Gran chuckled. "Don't fret over it. Not all marry the first they save, but you'll always be close. Always have a connection to them that you'll never have with another. No matter how many others you save." She fell silent a moment. "And if you ever lose them like I eventually did, since no human lives forever, then the dreams won't come as often. I'm glad we have another in the family. I worried about that. I won't live forever either."

Emily finally managed to think of something to say. "You're not dying for a long time, Gran." She stepped forward to hug the elderly woman.

Gran chuckled again, lightly patting her back. "Death comes for all humans eventually." She let go and took a step back. "Now get some sleep. There are things to do once the sun sets." She strode from the room.

Chapter Twenty

Emily stared at the empty doorway for a moment before she shook her head. It didn't help clear it. Turning away from the doorway, she got ready for bed, including setting the alarm to wake her before sunset.

She had no idea how long she slept before her usual nightmare made an appearance. She felt like screaming and telling her parents to stop invading her dreams. Before she could, they disappeared to be replaced by Cricket. The two of them stood in a pool of light cast by a streetlight. She stared down at the dog that looked up at her with a hopeful expression on his face.

"What do you want, boy?"

He wagged his tail.

"Why can't someone spell things out for me? Like with a big neon sign?"

Cricket barked once and ran off.

She stared into the darkness, hoping this wasn't going to be like the last dream Cricket had been in. Not far from her she noticed a billboard for health insurance. The backlit kind. That hadn't been what she'd wanted when she'd asked for a neon sign. Taking a step forward to follow Cricket, she was ripped from her dream by the beeping of the alarm clock.

"No." Keeping her eyes closed, she turned it off, trying to gather the threads of her dream and return to sleep. It didn't help. Sleep wasn't coming. She lay in the bed and stared at the ceiling. What if it had been important?

She guessed it couldn't be helped. The dream was lost and she had to get ready before the sun set and Essence came looking for her. She had no doubt he would. Before then she needed to be somewhere safe she could talk to him from. Somewhere he couldn't touch her.

It didn't take her long to get ready and join Dante in the kitchen for something to eat. Leo arrived not long after they'd eaten to tell them everything was organised on his end.

Emily's stomach slowly turned and she wondered

if she should have eaten. Taking a deep breath and rising to her feet, she met Leo's gaze. "I'm ready."

Dante stood beside her. "I'm ready too." He reached for her hand, threading his fingers between hers.

"I'll drop you at the cemetery."

With a hug for Gran, Emily followed Leo from the kitchen, Dante at her side. She collected her bow and a quiver of arrows on the way to Leo's vehicle. She already had daggers in her boots, vials of holy water in her pockets and had made sure Dante carried daggers and holy water too.

The drive to the cemetery was silent. She sat in the front and Dante was in the back. Outside the light faded, the sun setting as they reached the cemetery. She opened the door and stepped half out before she looked over her shoulder to Leo. "Thanks for the lift."

"Go with God." He clapped her on the back.

She nearly fell out of the vehicle, stumbling as she rose to her feet, taking her bow and quiver of arrows with her. Continuing to hold her bow and quiver, she reached for Dante's hand, holding on tightly as they walked inside the cemetery gates. They stopped not far in and turned to face the entrance. He wouldn't be long. He was sure to want to find out about her plan.

She didn't know what she'd do if he didn't agree. She had no Plan B.

When Essence arrived, she felt his power long before she saw him. It was like a wave going ahead of him. But there was something wrong with it. Or maybe right. Part of it didn't seem demonic. And that part seemed to have grown larger since the last time she'd spoken to him. Maybe they had more of a chance than she'd thought.

"Say your piece, hunter," Essence said.

She met his gaze, her shoulders back and her grip on Dante tight. "I have a plan. One that will destroy Donald. Financially and emotionally. People will curse his name for years. His and Susan's."

Essence inclined his head. "I'm listening."

Emily gathered her thoughts, recalling everything Gran had told her. She'd have one chance to get this right. One chance to convince Essence that her plan was the best. "We can't do this alone. I've arranged for help. People who believe and trust me and have offered their help without question."

"Will they do so again after tonight?"

She shrugged, already knowing the answer, but unable to say anything because he'd hear the lie in her words. Instead she told him her plan. The plan Gran had given her. When she finished she remained silent, waiting for him to speak. The silence stretched out and she began to think he might refuse. She fought for calmness, not wanting him to know how desperate she was for him to agree.

Essence gestured to the ground in front of them. "You will need to step out of sanctuary if you wish to go ahead with this."

"You do understand I'm not entering into any deals with you. This is a way we can take care of our common enemies," Emily said.

"You have told me more than enough times that you don't make deals with demons."

"But do you believe me?" She remained in sanctuary, waiting for him to tell her exactly what he was agreeing to.

"Once Donald has been taken care of I will come after both of you. One at a time."

"Susan needs to be dealt with too. Not just Donald."

"It will be done." He took a step back and to the side, gesturing for them to precede him.

Letting go of Dante's hand, Emily took out her phone and sent a text message. *Yes.* Not expecting a reply from Leo, she returned her phone to her pocket and once again took hold of Dante's hand. She dreaded stepping out of sanctuary. It was Dante who moved first and she stepped out with him, not wanting him to face Essence alone. They walked along the footpath beside Essence, stopping at a dark coloured sedan further up the street.

"The boy human can sit in the front." Essence opened the back door, looking to Emily. "You will sit in the back with me."

She tightened her grip on Dante's hand before letting go and getting in the car, resting her bow and quiver on the floor beside her. The driver had to be human, or if he was a demon he was so minor she couldn't tell around Essence's power. When Essence sat beside her, she had to force herself to remain seated and not open the other door and run. His power filled the car. Her plan was starting to feel like a really bad idea.

Staring out the window, she clasped her hands together in her lap. It had to work. This plan had to work. It had the greatest chance of success. Not that she knew exactly what that meant. She would have liked something more accurate, like percentages. If all other possible plans had a five percent chance of success, this one only needed to have a six percent chance to be the best option. Uneasiness spread through her and she forced herself to stop dwelling on percentages, success rates and all the things that could go wrong. She had to focus on surviving. On getting both her and Dante out of this situation alive.

The driver pulled up in front of a dark building, the street quiet and empty. Getting out of the car, she slung her quiver into place as she stared at the old brick building that stretched out in both directions. It was much bigger than she'd expected. Someone could easily get lost in a deserted building that size. Her grip on her bow tightened. This had to work.

Essence joined her on the footpath, knocking on the driver's window. He spoke the moment the window was lowered. "Fetch Susan and bring her here. If she objects tell her I'm not asking. Other than that, tell her nothing."

Dante took Emily's hand when he reached her side. "We should have brought a torch."

Essence held one out to Dante, a beam of light shining towards the building.

"Where did that come from?" Dante didn't take the torch.

"You don't want to know." Emily let go of his hand and took the torch rather than let Dante touch something that had been created with demonic power. "Let's do this." She strode towards the building, finding the front door unlocked. Stepping inside, she moved the beam of light around the room.

Broken office furniture, leaf litter and dirt was scattered across the floor. The uneasiness she'd felt when looking at the building, increased. This was not a good idea. She was in a deserted building with a demon far more powerful than any she'd ever encountered before. It wasn't even close to being a good idea.

"Anyone else could be in here, including homeless people," Dante said.

She didn't bother telling him it wasn't humans he needed to worry about. Anything could be in here. And they wouldn't know because Essence's power would mask it.

"If this is a trap for me, you will regret it," Essence said.

"Tonight is about trapping Donald and Susan." Midnight would bring with it another day. "I do plan to send you to hell, but it won't be tonight."

Essence cackled. "So you keep telling me, but here I am." He spread his arms wide. "More powerful than ever."

He might be more powerful, but there was definitely something wrong with his power. "Enjoy it while you can."

Essence cackled again. "I know you believe your

words. But believing in something doesn't automatically make it true."

"Nor does disbelieving it make it false." Not wanting to continue the conversation, she headed for the doorway that led further into the building, trying to remember all the directions she'd been given. Her footsteps echoed in the empty building, those of Dante's and Essence's sounding behind her. It was unnerving having a demon at her back. She wanted to look over her shoulder to see what he was doing. She managed to keep her gaze focused ahead of her until she reached the room they needed to be in. Looking towards him didn't help. Only made her more worried about everything.

Dragging her gaze away from Essence, she shone the torch around the room. It wasn't much cleaner than the first room they'd been in. The only difference was this room contained a lot of old industrial equipment. Some of it was intact, but the majority of it was damaged, many of it towering over her in the high-ceilinged room.

Essence grabbed hold of Dante's arm, dragging him towards some of the equipment, a chain appearing in his hand.

Dante tried to pull out of Essence's grip. "I can walk without help."

Essence ignored him, pushing him roughly against the equipment and chaining his hands to it.

Emily wanted to protest Essence's actions. She pressed her lips tightly together in an effort not to speak. She'd agreed on the plan. It was too late now to back out of it. Not wanting Essence to take her bow and quiver from her, she found a spot out of the way, near the door, putting them behind some of the equipment. Turning around, she saw Essence coming towards her, another length of chain in his hand. She wanted to run. Instead, she walked towards him. "We need better lighting than a single torch."

Several of the bare bulbs hanging down low from the ceiling lit up with an unnatural glow. "You are very demanding, hunter." With a look from Essence, the torch vanished from Emily's hands.

He grabbed her roughly and she bit back her protests. He was a demon, she doubted he knew how to be nice. When he chained her up at the opposite end of the room to Dante, she fought against panic. It was bad enough that they needed to be chained, but being separated by so much space felt worse. Which was illogical. If anything was to happen it wouldn't matter how close she was to Dante if her hands were chained. "How far away is Susan?"

Chapter Twenty-One

Essence held out his hands, curved daggers appearing in each one. "She has entered the building." His lips twisted into an unnerving smile. "Time to see how obedient my human is."

Emily's stomach lurched. The plan had to work.

Susan strode into the room a minute later, following the driver. She looked annoyed. "Will this take long? I have other things to do."

Essence crossed the room to stand in front of her. "It will take as long as I say and you'll be here for as long as I wish."

Susan lowered her head, her expression becoming neutral. "Of course, Essence. I apologise for being impatient." She clasped her hands together in front of her, head remaining bowed. "Is there anything I can do for you?"

Emily fought against the pity she felt for the

woman. There were other choices she could have made. Back when Essence had been weak.

"Bring your grandfather here."

"He won't come."

"You will convince him."

"He's terrified you'll kill him."

Essence shifted the daggers to one hand, reaching out to run his hand along her cheek, continuing downwards. He stopped at her throat, his hand splayed across it. "You will convince him. Because he let the hunters get hold of my power, it has been damaged. I can no longer kill those who damaged it. I need another to do it. Your grandfather."

"You can gather essence and power for yourself. Now you have your own power back you'll be able to do something with the power you collect. Why do you need him to kill the children?"

"That isn't what this is about. Bring your grandfather here. If you don't convince him to come, I will hold you personally responsible for everything that has gone wrong. You were the one who chose the boy human."

Seeing the fear in Susan's eyes, Emily wanted to tell Essence to stop. That this wasn't right. She pressed her lips together tightly, her hands curling into fists.

Maybe others would forgive her for this night, but she didn't know if she'd be able to forgive herself.

Susan remained completely still. "I can do it for you. Let me kill them."

"Only your grandfather can end the life of the boy human. Tell him I want him here. Tell him that if I don't have to hunt him down I'll let him live."

"You won't kill him?"

"No."

"You won't ask another to kill him? He's the only family I have left."

"Once you called me family."

Emily shivered at the tone of Essence's voice. There seemed to be a threat in it.

"He's my only human family left." Susan spoke the words quickly. "You won't ask another to kill him?"

"If he dies it won't be at my hand or my command." Essence removed his hand from her neck. "Bring him to me. Now."

"Yes, Master." Susan hurried from the room, head still bowed.

Essence waved for the driver to follow her before striding over to Emily.

She kept her gaze on his eyes, not wanting to focus on the daggers he held in his left hand. "How long will it take her to find him?"

"She knows where he is. She always does."

"How long?"

"He has a place that is blessed to protect him against demons and secured against humans. It was where he was running to with my power when you stole it from him. He'll soon learn nowhere is safe for him. It's half an hour away."

"Then we don't need to be chained for now."

Essence cackled. "There's no need to set you free." He strode from the room.

Emily stared after him, her teeth gritted together as she tried not to yell after him to let them go. Her hands curled into fists and she tugged at the chains wrapped around her wrists. Why had she thought this plan was a good idea? Being chained and powerless was one of the worst feelings. No wonder demons hated being powerless.

"Emily-"

Worried he might say something Essence shouldn't hear, she interrupted. "He hasn't gone far."

"There's nothing I have to say he can't hear."

He had no idea and she hadn't had the time to teach him. "It's surprising the amount of things you should avoid letting demons know about."

"Like what?"

A half smile formed. "Many things." She paused,

wishing she could see Dante properly. There was too much in the way for her to be able to see more than parts of him. "If you didn't know I was a hunter, I'd want to tell you. I'd want to convince you of the truth." There was a long silence and she tugged against the chains, trying to see him. From what Gran had said, she was starting to believe the only reason she'd had her second premonition was because Dante had been in danger. Otherwise, why had it taken six months?

"I would want to tell you too."

She couldn't stop a grin from forming. Didn't want to. "We'll return him to hell. Once everything else is dealt with."

"Yes."

They remained silent and Emily stared at everything she could see, checking where it was and making sure she knew the layout of the room as much as she possibly could from her position. If it came down to a fight she wanted to have the best chance of winning. She really hoped it didn't come to one in this room. Not with how crowded it was. She was wishing she could reach her pockets to check the time on her phone when she heard footsteps and sensed Essence rapidly coming towards the room from a different direction to the sound.

She wanted to say something to Dante. Wish him luck or repeat her earlier words, but she couldn't. Not with how close everyone was. Susan stepped into the room first, Donald following her, the driver behind him.

Donald looked around the room, his head turning jerkily in each direction. "Where is he? Are you sure I'm safe?"

"I've already told you. He said he wouldn't kill you. Or have anyone else do it for him." Susan smiled. "I keep telling you he cares."

"And I keep telling you you're a fool. The only thing that demon cares about is power. His power."

Essence entered the room. "You're wrong."

With a yelp Donald scurried behind Susan, who gave him a daggered look, her lips thinning.

Essence smiled at Donald's reaction. "I care about revenge and myself as well."

Donald glared at Susan, an accusation in his eyes. "I knew it. I knew he wanted me dead."

Essence slowly shook his head, walking towards Donald. "I don't want you dead." He gestured in Dante's direction. "I want him dead. That is the revenge I was talking about. You are going to kill him for me."

Emily took a deep breath, needing to say the words

she'd mentally rehearsed several times. "Not Dante. Don't hurt him. He didn't do anything. I'm the one to blame." She waited for the words Essence was meant to say.

He gave a dagger to Susan and one to Donald, his gaze turning to Emily. "Do you admit it? Are you the reason my power has been corrupted?"

She held his gaze. Those weren't the words he was meant to have said. Uneasiness turned into fear. "You can't kill Dante. Let him go. He isn't a part of this." Six percent came to mind. Was it possible to have waking premonitions? If she managed to get out of this, she'd have to ask Gran.

"You didn't answer the question." Essence strode towards her, stopping right in front of her. "Are you guilty?"

She had a really bad feeling about what might happen if she answered the question. She was guilty and he'd hear it whether she told the truth or lied. "Let's talk about guilt." She looked past him to Susan, needing to get the conversation back where it was meant to be. "Who killed my parents?"

Susan laughed. "Is that what all this is about? Is that why you came after me and rescued him?" She gestured in the direction of Dante. "You should have left well enough alone. You're a child. Did you really think you could take on demons?"

Mindful that others should be listening, ones who weren't hunters, Emily said, "Demons? Just because someone wears a mask and a suit and calls himself one, doesn't make him a demon. Did you kill my parents?" She hoped there were others listening or all this would have been for nothing. They were meant to have followed Donald into the building.

Susan shrugged. "There have been so many over the years. I don't suppose you were considerate enough to bring a picture for me."

The woman's tone of voice destroyed every little bit of sympathy she'd felt for her. "Did he make you kill all of them?" She glanced towards Essence before returning her gaze to Susan.

Susan stepped forward so she was standing beside Essence. "He taught me the benefits." She looked Emily up and down. "You think your beauty will last? Your youth? One day lines will start around your eyes letting you know death is creeping closer. Then you'll start noticing them elsewhere. Why would I let myself die when I have Essence to help me live forever? I've done all he's asked and more." A mocking smile momentarily appeared. "So much more."

The smile made Emily want to look away. There'd been something demonic about it. An expression that should never be seen on a human face. "I have a picture of them."

Susan laughed. "Are you serious? You carry a photo around? Do you ask everyone you see if they killed your parents?"

"It's on my phone. In my right pocket. It's the background picture."

Susan retrieved the phone and stared at it. "They seem familiar." She was quiet a moment. "I know who they are. They thought they could come in and mess things up." Smiling, Susan tossed the phone to the floor. It landed near Emily's feet. "I taught them how wrong they were." Susan stepped forward and pressed the dagger against Emily's throat. "Just like I'll teach you how wrong you are."

"No." Essence put his hand on Susan's shoulder, but didn't move her away. "Together. Kill the humans together."

Emily continued to stare into Susan's blue eyes. It took her a moment to recognise what she saw. Excitement. Anticipation. And she couldn't do anything about it because she'd allowed the demon to chain her up. Kicking out at Susan might gain her a couple of minutes, but it'd only postpone the inevitable. She was trapped.

"Hurry up, grandfather. Don't tell me you're growing remorseful in your old age. After all you were the one who first taught me about human sacrifice and demons." Susan continued to stare into Emily's eyes as she spoke.

Emily heard footsteps, wishing she could look away and see if it was Donald. Instead she continued to meet Susan's gaze. Blue eyes set in a face with flawless skin.

"You're so pretty." Susan spoke in a wistful whisper. "And so young."

"I'm ready," Donald called out.

Smiling, Susan drew back the hand with the dagger. "I will have it all. Your beauty and your youth."

An arrow shot the dagger from Susan's hand and a few seconds later a man called out, "Police. Drop your weapons and put your hands where we can see them." Armed men came in the door.

Emily didn't feel in the least bit relieved to see them. Her and Dante were chained up and anything could happen. Plans didn't always work out.

Susan screamed, more anger than fear in the sound, dropping to her knees to pick up the dagger. A police officer came forward and grabbed hold of her, kicking the dagger out of the way.

Essence's wings snapped out and he sped across the room towards Dante, ignoring all the warnings to freeze. Several gunshots rang out and Emily struggled against the chains preventing her from helping. She sensed Essence's power heading towards the front of the building. The moment he walked out the front door the unnatural glow vanished from the bulbs. A figure dropped down beside her seconds before the lights went out, dressed in black and wearing a balaclava, a quiver and bow slung across his back.

"You're safe, Emily."

She recognised Leo's voice and spoke equally as soft, desperate to escape and help Dante. "Get this chain off me."

"I'm working on it." There was a snapping sound, barely heard over the noise in the rest of the room as torches were turned on and officers handcuffed Susan, Donald and the driver. Susan wasn't going quietly.

As soon as the chains fell away, Emily picked up her phone and started to head towards Dante.

Chapter Twenty-Two

Leo grabbed hold of Emily's arm, drawing her in the opposite direction. "Adam is going after Dan. This way. We need to avoid attention."

"Why do you get all the crazy ones, Tuck?" one of the officers asked.

"I guess I'm extremely lucky," Tuck said dryly.

"Not what I would have called it," the officer who had Donald said.

"You were cutting it a bit close there." An officer walking past Tuck said to him. "I thought the girl was about to be killed. It wouldn't have been fun trying to explain that in a report."

Emily was glad of the shadows and the equipment in the room. There was no way she could answer any questions.

"Did someone get the kids?" another officer asked. "Where are they?"

"And what was with that arrow? Who fired it? Why aren't we looking for them?" the officer who'd mentioned crazy ones asked.

Emily picked up her bow and quiver as they reached them, wondering if she should leave them behind after that last comment. Her hand tightened on her bow. No, she couldn't bring herself to do that. She followed Leo into the corridor, wishing there was light when she ran into him. Hearing voices behind her, she instantly changed her mind.

"In here." Leo pulled her into the next room along the corridor.

"What about Dante and Adam?" She tensed when she heard a sound at the doorway.

"Leo?" Adam whispered.

"We're in here."

"He wasn't there."

Fear rushed in on her and her legs nearly gave out at Adam's words. "Who wasn't there?" She willed him to say another name.

"Dan."

Her eyes closed and she wanted to scream the same way Susan had. "Where is he?"

"Essence must have him," Adam said. "The links of the chain was scattered across the floor near where he'd been."

Slinging her quiver and bow on her back, she rubbed at her demon mark, trying to think what to do. There were no demons in the area. Dante had trusted her. Believed that she'd save him. Her dream rushed in on her. "I need Cricket. I need him brought here now."

"Emily, we have to-"

She interrupted Leo. "I need Cricket. He was in my dream."

"Detective Tuck said we couldn't stick around. That he couldn't keep us out of it if we stayed. He didn't like the idea that we were using kids as bait so I'm pretty sure he won't be helpful if we're caught here," Leo said. "It took a lot to convince him it was the only way to save the pair of you."

"I can't leave Dante with Essence." She stared at the indistinct figure of her uncle, not speaking the words she really wanted to say. *He loves me.* How could she cope with losing someone else she loved? The pain of losing her parents washed over her and she forced it away. She couldn't think about them. She had to focus on Dante.

"We'll get out of the building then figure out what to do." Leo took hold of her upper arm. "This way." He drew her towards a broken window, letting her go to climb out on a fairly wide ledge.

Looking outside, Emily saw the ledge ran across the building, swallowed by the darkness. She took Leo's hand and climbed outside, inching along the building, needing to face the wall because of the bow and quiver on her back. She noticed her uncles had to do the same. "Who shot the dagger from Susan's hand?"

"Me," Adam said. "It was the signal to Detective Tuck. I was surprised he managed to last that long and not step in. He's a good bloke."

"But don't forget he's a cop first," Leo warned. "If he catches us around here, he will take us in for questioning." Reaching a fire escape, Leo jumped onto it and started for the ground.

Emily followed. The moment she was on the ground, she took out her phone. She was about to find out how good her protective case was. "Who's at your place? Who can bring Cricket here?"

"Saul." Leo placed a hand on her shoulder. "Are you sure this is what you want to do? Not just the building, but the surrounding area could be full of police soon."

"Yeah. I dreamt of Cricket. I just didn't know why until now." She dialled Saul's phone number, relieved when her own worked.

Saul answered before the first ring ended. "Did everything go well?"

"No. I need Cricket."

"Is Leo with you?"

She sighed, wishing Saul could have said yes without needing to talk to his brother. She held her phone out to Leo, wanting to tell him to hurry up.

"Bring the dog." Leo gave directions and disconnected the call before he returned the phone to Emily. "We'll wait a street over. That's where we're parked."

She didn't want to leave the building, but she knew the direction Essence had initially taken. That would be close enough. "Okay."

They waited in the vehicle, sitting in darkness, all of them remaining silent. Emily was on the back seat, her bow and quiver beside her. She wanted to take them with her. Wanted to have her favourite weapon when she tracked Essence down. But she'd leave them behind and hope she needed nothing more than the daggers in her boots and the vials of holy water in her pockets.

A vehicle pulled up behind them and Saul got out, opening the back door. Cricket jumped from the vehicle and ran over to Emily, who'd stepped onto the footpath the moment she'd seen them. She bent to pat the dog, feeling like she should apologise to him for losing his owner. The glow of a billboard caught her attention, her breath catching in her throat. She hadn't noticed it before because of the direction they'd come from. It was an advertisement for health insurance.

"It's all over the news. I was listening to the radio on the way here." Saul gestured in the direction of the building. "I hope you don't need to go over there. It's crawling with people."

Emily took a deep breath, taking the lead rope Saul held out to her. "No. I have a place I can start from." A neon sign. If she'd read the clue correctly. She clipped the lead rope to Cricket's collar, looking at each of her uncles. "I have to do this alone."

"We will be tracking you," Leo warned. "You won't really be alone."

She smiled slightly. "Thank you." Looking down at Cricket, she tightened her grip on the lead. She wasn't about to let him disappear on her like he had a tendency to do in her dreams. "Come on, boy." She strode towards the sign, thinking of her other uncles. Taking out her phone she rang Ian.

"Are you okay?" There was fear in his voice.

"Sorry. I thought you'd want to know there's something on the news you might be interested in."

"Give me a minute."

"I can't chat. There's a couple more things I have to deal with."

"The cult? That's the news you wanted me to listen to? With the blond chick and the old man?"

"Yeah, that's them."

"I wish we'd done more than destroyed his house."

She didn't blame him, nor was she surprised by the anger in his voice. The billboard was only metres away. "I have to go, Uncle Ian."

There was a few seconds of silence, the news report playing in the background. "You're following in their footsteps, aren't you? Taking after your parents."

"Yeah."

"Don't go getting yourself killed. Whatever it is you're up to. Darren once told me he might tell me about it when I learned not to take so many risks."

She could hear the question in his words and couldn't prevent laughter from escaping. "That sounds like Dad." Maybe one day she'd tell him, but it wouldn't be any time soon.

"I miss him. Every day."

"Me too. Both of them." She couldn't have this conversation right now. Not while Dante was with Essence. "I'll see you soon. For dinner one night."

"It's a deal. Let me know when."

"I will." She disconnected the call, staring at the time on the phone. A chill ran through her. Two forty-five a.m. Her hand tightened on her phone and she returned it to her pocket before she threw it at something. She was sick of seeing that time. In an effort to distract herself, she thought of the phone call. She'd take Dante with her to dinner. Ian wouldn't mind. She smiled slightly at the irony of the word he'd used. A deal. That was the kind of deal she was willing to make. Ones with demons were another matter. The only things she was willing to give them was promises. And she'd made one to Essence she was planning to keep. He was headed for hell. Him and his power. She wanted him to be stuck there for a very long time.

Stopping at the billboard, she crouched in front of Cricket. "I need you to find Dante. You did it before. Remember? When they grabbed him while the two of you were taking a walk." She willed the dog to move. Willed him to start looking. "Where's Dante? Come on, boy. Where is he?" She rose to her feet. "Dante. Find Dante." He didn't move, only looked up at her, his tail wagging. Her heart sank. She'd been so certain this was what her dream had meant.

Crouching in front of Cricket again, she rubbed his

head. "He needs help. He's in danger. The same ones have him. Please, Cricket. Find Dante."

Cricket licked her hand, his tail continuing to wag.

She closed her eyes, trying to remember everything about the dream. Cricket had run off. Without a lead. Opening her eyes, she stared at him. "Don't leave me behind, okay?" Unclipping the lead, she stood. The dog didn't move. About to demand what else could she do, she watched open-mouthed as Cricket started sniffing around. She closed her mouth, remaining silent.

He stayed in the one spot for a little longer and gave a single bark before running down the street.

She ran after him, trying to keep up. It was only that he stopped every now and then to sniff the ground that she didn't lose sight of him. They went down street after street and she began to wish she had a motorbike. A car wouldn't have helped since he cut through areas where one wouldn't have been able to go. She was starting to wonder how far they'd gone when she sensed it. Essence's power. And she was slowly getting closer to it.

Cricket led her to a house that was in darkness, a streetlight out the front showing an overgrown yard and a missing front door, graffiti sprayed across the outside walls. Normally she'd think twice before going into a house like that. Actually, she'd think more than twice and probably decide not to take another step closer. But she doubted anyone would be stupid enough to be around here tonight. Those that ignored the chill up their spine from Essence's power probably wouldn't see morning. Pushing that unnerving thought away, she strode towards the front door, Cricket at her side. She didn't blame him for not wanting to run off.

Pausing at the front door, she looked down at the dog. Dante wouldn't want anything to happen to him. As much as she feared walking in there alone, she didn't want anything to happen to him either. "Stay, boy." She pointed to the ground. "Stay." She took a step inside, glancing back to see that he remained in place. Facing forward, she peered into the darkness, wishing she had a torch. As she reached for her phone to use the screen for light, the ceiling bulb glowed with the unnatural light Essence had created in the abandoned building.

Essence stood across the room from her. "I knew you'd come after him. You hunters are so predictable like that."

Chapter Twenty-Three

A glance around the room showed Emily they were alone. Her heart lurched when she spied Dante's phone amongst the empty beer bottles and broken furniture. "I promised you a trip to hell." But first she needed to find Dante.

Essence cackled. "And I told you it takes more than believing your words to make them true."

"Where's Dante?"

"You have more things to worry about than where the boy human is."

The way he spoke the words had her tilting her head slightly to the side. "I thought you'd have killed him by now." Not that she wanted that to happen, but there'd definitely been something odd about the tone of his voice.

"He will die. Eventually."

A slight smile formed. She wondered if Gran had

known when she'd suggested the excuse for them to tell Susan. "But not by you." The relief she felt was short lived.

Essence was across the room in seconds, slamming her against the wall near the door. "What do you know? Tell me what he did."

Cricket stood in the doorway, growling warningly.

The scent of demon washed over her and she didn't know what to do. Her heart raced and she feared she wouldn't see sunrise. She met his gaze, trying to remain still. "Let me go. I can't help you until I've spoken to Dante. I don't know what he did." But whatever it was, she wasn't about to undo it so Essence could kill him.

The demon kept hold of her. "If that dog attacks me, I will destroy it."

"Then let go of me. He doesn't like the way you're threatening me." She tried to keep her voice steady. Tried not to panic at being held against a wall by a demon so powerful it made her breath continually freeze in her throat, the scent of him overpowering.

"What did the boy human do?" He didn't loosen his grip.

"I've already told you. You should be able to hear I'm not lying. Let me go and I'll ask him." She watched his expression, wishing she could tell what the changes on his feline like face meant. "Let me go."

He released her so suddenly she collapsed on the floor near the lead she'd dropped when he'd slammed her against the wall. "Find out. Now."

She stared up at him, pushing Cricket away when he tried to lick her face. Opening her mouth to speak, she instantly closed it. He couldn't tell if she was lying. She was almost certain of it. Slowly getting to her feet, she tried to push Cricket outside. He wasn't moving from where he leaned against her. She looked down at him long enough to speak. "Out." He didn't move and she didn't want to take her attention off Essence for more than a few seconds. "I need to tie him up so he doesn't get in the way." She picked up the lead, clipped it onto Cricket's collar and stepped outside. It didn't take long to tie him to the fence. "Stay. Be safe." She patted his head, ignoring his whining as she walked away. She paused in the doorway, having no clue what to do next. Stalling for time wouldn't help. Sunrise wasn't close enough for that to work.

Essence gestured towards the doorway he'd used to enter the room. "He's that way."

Emily took a step into the room. "It seems a little

one-sided to expect me to help you and yet you plan to kill me today."

"Are you finally ready to make a deal with a demon?"

"Of course not. I'm a hunter." She met his gaze, planning to lie to him. "But I won't try and send you to hell today if you were to let Dante and me leave this house without any further harm."

"And in exchange you are to ask Dante what he did."

She nodded, not liking how unequal his offer was. "That seems fair." She continued to watch him, seeing no change in his expression. She kept her own neutral when all she wanted to do was cheer.

"He's down the hallway to the left. In the far bedroom."

She bit her lip in an effort to contain her excitement. He'd believed her. Believed her when she'd deliberately lied. When had he lost the ability to hear truth and lies? When his power had returned to him or when the corruption had grown? "Okay." Keeping an eye on him, she crossed the room and stepped into the hallway. It went to both the left and the right. The ceiling light bulb glowed with the same eerie light as the one in the first room.

Hearing him behind her, she turned to the left

and strode to the last room, the light bulb starting to glow as she reached it. She stopped in the doorway, a sense of déjà vu washing over her when she saw Dante chained to a solid metal bed frame, his gaze meeting hers. This one had no mattress or linen, but it brought to mind the night they'd met. She wanted to run across the room when she saw the blood and bruising on him. She held herself still, turning to face Essence, keeping her voice low. "Give me some time to convince him. Without you hovering over us. He's not likely to say anything with you nearby."

"You have ten minutes."

She slowly shook her head. "You really overestimate us humans sometimes. And yet at others you completely underestimate us. I need more than ten minutes."

"Fifteen." He strode away before she could speak.

"What have you done, Em?"

She turned to face Dante. "Don't you trust me?"

He smiled. "Of course I do. But the question's still the same."

She crossed the room and sat beside him on the bed, the metal cold through her jeans. "I should have brought my lock picks."

"He tried to kill me."

"What happened?" She leaned close to him to hear his soft words.

"He materialised one of those curved daggers he likes." He remained silent for a moment. "I seriously thought that was it. And yet I stood there staring at him when I should have been doing something else. Fighting back, running, anything." He shrugged. "I don't know what, but anything other than standing there and waiting for him to kill me."

"What happened?" She kept her voice equally soft wanting to ask him to hurry up. They had very little time.

He shrugged. "I seriously don't know. I saw the blade coming for me and it stopped. Centimetres from my face. It stopped like there was something between me and the blade." He paused a moment. "Why aren't I dead?"

"I don't know. What did you do when you released his power? Exactly what you did. What you were thinking, what you said, everything."

"I was terrified he'd kill you. I removed my cross from the cord and holding it in one hand and the box latch with the other muttered, 'Let this work. By whatever gods are around, let this work.' Then I opened the box and dropped the cross in. I felt the power rush over my hand, but didn't see anything. The cross was lying in the bottom of an empty box."

She leaned her head against him, closing her eyes for a moment.

"Em?" He waited until she looked at him before he spoke. "What did I do?"

A half smile escaped. "Crazy stuff."

"Like?"

"There are creatures that answer to being called god. Even some demons answer that call, but I don't think it was a demon. There is a part of his power that is nothing like him. Those other creatures are as old as demons and can be just as powerful. There's a good chance you invoked one of them with your chant and the power you held in your hand."

"What does that mean?"

"It's trapped in him too. And I bet it wants his power."

"Is that good or bad?"

"I don't know. But I do know it saved your life."

"Can we use that?"

She tilted her head slightly. "I don't know. But we also have one other trick up our sleeve."

"What's that?"

"He can't tell when we lie."

"Since when?"

"I'm guessing it's been since he gained a hitchhiker or since his hitchhiker has continued to corrupt his power." She frowned. "Or taken the corruption from it."

Dante laughed softly. "A hitchhiker inside a demon. That's a scary image."

"Yeah." Normally it was the other way around. A demon invading the body of another and trying to take control.

"What are we going to tell him?"

She felt her lips curve as an idea came to her. "We need to be apart. You have to ask your new friend to tell me what he wants. I need to know if he plans to do something evil with the power. Or if he'll keep it safe and away from Essence."

"How will that help?"

"We can return Essence to hell and summon him. His power will remain behind until he can bring it out. Through things like sacrifice."

"How do I ask him?"

"The same way you did the first time." She held his gaze. "Do you trust me?"

He reached for her, running his hand along her cheek and threading his fingers through her hair as he slid his hand to the nape of her neck. "With my life." He drew her close, his lips meeting hers.

Emily clung to him, returning his kiss, not pulling away until she heard Essence walking down the hallway. "We can do this." She rose to her feet, taking a step backwards, meeting Dante's gaze. "I'm certain of it."

"What are you certain of?" Essence stood in the doorway.

Emily crossed the room to stand in front of him. "Dante isn't completely certain what he did. But I think I know." She held out her hand. "I get visions sometimes. Let's see what comes to me. Take my hand so I can figure this out for sure and then I can tell you how to fix your power." She held his gaze. "Why are you hesitating? I know you can hear when I'm telling a lie, so why would I even bother trying to lie to you? What's the problem?"

Essence took her hand. "Tomorrow I will come after you. Both of you. This is only a reprieve."

"You have to be able to find us first." She held his gaze a moment longer before closing her eyes, trying to ignore the feel of his leathery skin and the demonic scent of him.

It took several minutes before she heard the whispers. They didn't make sense. She concentrated, trying to figure out what the creature was saying. Sleep? Surely it wasn't saying sleep. Undisturbed?

Neither word made sense. A feeling of being dragged from somewhere dark and deep underground washed over her. Being forced against the creature's will to do a human's bidding. Struggling against losing itself to the demon.

"I'm sorry." She didn't realise she'd spoken aloud until Essence spoke.

"What are you sorry about?"

She opened her eyes, letting go of his hand. "He didn't mean it." She spoke the words to the creature, not the demon. Hopefully the creature would realise that. "There's only one way to fix this problem."

"How?"

"You must return to hell and be called back here." The creature wouldn't be forced to stay in hell. It wasn't from there. The moment it was separated from Essence, it would be able to leave.

Essence stared at her a moment. "Hell?" When she nodded, he slammed her against the wall. "You tricked me." His face was close to hers, anger in his eyes and voice.

"Let her go." Dante leapt from the bed. The metal feet scraped against the floor as he tried to reach her, the bed moving a fraction at a time.

Emily fought against the fear that wanted to overwhelm her, her body aching from the impact.

"Listen to my words. This is the truth. You can hear it, can't you?" She doubted he'd admit that he couldn't.

His grip didn't loosen. "Of course I can hear the truth in your words. Lies as well. Say the words again. Tell me your plan."

Chapter Twenty-Four

Emily held herself completely still, barely daring to breathe. "I'll send you to hell and call you straight back. Once the power is separated from you, what Dante did to it will be undone. You'll be free of the corruption." And the creature would be free to take the power far from Essence's reach.

"You want me here, powerless. That's what all this is about, isn't it?"

"No. You'll gain it quickly enough. There are others who would do your bidding. Ones like Susan."

"How long would it be until you called me back?"

"Immediately." She continued to hold his gaze, willing him to believe her.

"What were you wanting in return?"

"I do not make deals with demons. But it would be considered fair for you not to harm either of us the first day you returned to Earth."

"Who will be here when I return?"

She didn't dare look past him to Dante, who'd stopped trying to move the bed. "No more than those who are already here." She could feel morning approaching. "The sun will rise soon and when you're forced to wait for the evening, we'll escape and you'll never have the chance of this offer again. It has to be the two of us who send you back. If it's anyone else, what Dante accidentally did will not be undone." He had to agree. Someone else might realise the truth and tell him what would really happen.

Essence's grip tightened on her, pressing her more firmly against the wall before releasing her and stepping back. "You will be the first who dies when I return." He pointed his clawed finger at her. "When I go hunting on the second day it'll be you I come after." An expression very similar to Susan's, when she'd waited to kill Emily, crossed his face. "There will be no mercy."

"You have to find me first." She refused to look away from his gaze even though the power behind it caused fear to race through her and her legs struggle to hold her up.

"I will find you." The words hung in the air a moment before he spoke again. "Send me home."

"Remove the chain from Dante first."

Essence cackled. "And have two of you to deal with when I return? He doesn't need to be free. Now send me home."

Emily moved to stand beside Dante, linking her fingers through his. "Don't fight it. Let the words send you back or I'll be forced to use holy water."

"It will go very badly for you if you do. Say your prayer. Nothing more."

She spoke the words of the Lord's Prayer, continuing to grip Dante's hand. She doubted she could have remembered any other prayer than the one she'd said the most throughout her life. It'd been the first one her parents had taught her. Watching Essence, she saw him struggle against the words. She'd nearly reached the end, fearing it would take more than a prayer to send him back, when he vanished. The light bulb went out. Relief washed over her and she turned to Dante, pressing her lips to his, wrapping her arms around him. They were alive. Somehow, they were still alive.

Dante held onto her. "What do we do now?"

"Get these chains off you." Pulling away from him she took out her phone and rang Leo, light starting to filter into the room through the dirty window.

"You got rid of him? I no longer feel him in the area."

"Not quite. Can you come and get some chains off Dante? And probably collect Cricket."

"I'll be there in a minute."

She slid her phone into a pocket when he disconnected.

"Cricket is here?"

Emily nodded. "He helped me find you." The corners of her mouth tilted up. "I dreamt he would."

Dante chuckled. "See, I said you'd dream my location if you lost me."

Sobering, she framed his face with her hands. "You can't imagine how I felt when I realised he'd taken you."

"Easily. All I'd have to do is think how I'd feel if he'd taken you."

Cricket barked, followed by Leo calling out. "Where are you?"

She let go of Dante, walking backwards to the door, her gaze still on him, dim light filling the room from the rising sun. "I'll be back in a second." Turning, she hurried out the front to where Leo crouched by Cricket, patting him on the head. "This way."

"What exactly is going on?"

She filled Leo in on the basics, continuing to tell him as he cut the chain with a pair of bolt cutters.

When the chain fell to the ground, Dante rubbed at his wrist. "The creature wants his power."

"Why?" That didn't sound good to her.

"So others can't disturb it. The creature wants to return to its haven deep in the ground. It plans to use the power to protect itself from others who might call on it."

"Are you certain that's the only reason it wants power?" Leo asked.

"Yes. It was extremely annoyed I forced it to link up with a demon when they're enemies. I don't know what it is or even if it's male or female," Dante said.

"I don't think they have a gender." Leo looked from one to the other. "Is there anything else you need before we call Essence back?"

Emily held out her left hand and Leo clasped it so their demon marks touched. "I've got this. All I need is my bow and arrows."

"You don't have to do this on your own."

Letting go of him, she glanced towards Dante with a half smile. "I won't be on my own."

Leo also glanced towards Dante. "He isn't trained."

"He's trained enough to be able to throw vials of holy water at a demon."

"It's nearly impossible to quit, isn't it?" Leo smiled fleetingly. "Your gear is in my vehicle."

They followed Leo outside and Emily collected her gear and more vials of holy water while Dante made a fuss over Cricket. He put Cricket in the back of the vehicle and the two of them stood side-by-side, watching as Leo drove away. They returned inside, remaining in the first room.

Dante looked around, picking up his phone when he spotted it, sliding it into a pocket of his jeans. "How do we do this?"

"Summoning a demon is far easier than most people realise. Especially when that demon is waiting for your call." She gestured towards the blood staining his shirt. "Can I use your blood since he already has it?" It felt good to know exactly what to do after so many days of uncertainty.

Removing his shirt, Dante held it out to her. "Now what?"

She couldn't resist taking a few seconds to admire his chest. When her gaze returned to his face, he was grinning. She supposed she couldn't blame him. "Let's create a nice little surprise for him." Taking out one of the vials of holy water, she sprinkled it over the floor before putting the shirt on it. She moved away from where she'd placed it in the centre of the room, readying her bow and arrow. "Stay clear."

Dante moved closer to her. "What do I do other than throw holy water at him?"

"That'll be more than enough. Unless you remember the words of the prayer I said earlier."

Dante shook his head. "Not likely."

"The holy water will be enough then. You ready for a bit of craziness?"

"Crazy?" He grinned at her. "I hadn't realised."

She felt like cheering at what he was telling her. Instead, she drew in a deep breath and slowly released it. "Okay, let's do this." She took another deep breath. "Essence, I summon you from hell. I have placed blood before me for you. Come and take my offering." She said the words twice more, drawing back the arrow when Essence materialised in front of her, cursing the holy water on the ground where he stood. She released the arrow.

"You said you wouldn't attack me." Essence ripped the arrow from his shoulder, throwing it on the floor.

"I lied." She fired a second arrow at him while Dante threw an open vial of holy water.

Essence roared, grabbing for the bloodstained shirt. She shot his hand, trying to force him to drop the shirt. He screamed from the pain of the arrow, but continued to bring the shirt to his lips. Before she had the chance to shoot him again or for Dante to throw another vial of holy water at him, Essence pressed the bloodstain to his lips. He roared, cursing Emily while Dante gasped from pain, his hand pressed against the wall to steady himself.

Essence threw the shirt on the floor. "What have you done to me? Why didn't that work? Why can't I feel any of my power?"

Dante straightened, letting go of the wall. "You having problems, Essence?"

Essence pointed at Emily. "You. What did you do to me?"

"Didn't the blood work?"

"You know it didn't. I can hear it in your voice."

She guessed it must have been the creature preventing him from hearing her lies. "Are you having trouble drawing some of your power through from hell?" She couldn't resist asking him.

"What did you do?" His wings snapped open and he rushed towards them.

Before he'd barely moved, Emily punctured his wings with four arrows and he dropped to the ground, the wings closing. "Return to hell. Permanently."

"You can't do that to me." He roared again, a vial of holy water hitting him, the liquid running down his body. He clawed at the spot, trying to come towards them, arrows preventing him from making progress.

"Let no one call you from hell. Let no power return to you." She fired the last of her arrows into his body. Dropping her bow, she took the two daggers from her boots.

"I will escape and I will come after you."

She held the dagger, closest to Dante, towards him. "Holy water."

He tipped it over the blade, taking out another vial.

"Other demons owe me favours." Essence ran towards Emily.

She dodged to the side, striking out at him with her daggers. "Let your favours be owed to the one who holds your power. Let no more favours be paid to you."

When he failed to get Emily, Essence turned his attention to Dante, his claws raking across Dante's shoulders as he tried to escape.

Chapter Twenty-Five

Emily got between Essence and Dante, sinking her blades into the demon before drawing them out and slipping out of the way of his attack. "Stay back, Dante." Essence might have lost his power, but he was still a demon and far stronger than humans.

"Can you do that? Everything you said?" Dante retreated to the doorway.

"I can only pray and hope that someone answers my prayers." She began, using the same prayer as earlier. Again and again she attacked Essence with the daggers, her words ringing out in the room. He faltered as she neared the end of the prayer, vanishing before she reached the final words. She continued anyway, standing in the middle of the room as she spoke them. Wanting to do everything possible to ensure Essence never returned.

Dante came to stand beside her when she finished,

staring at the spot Essence had vanished from. "All hope abandon, ye who enter here."

She started to laugh, unable to stop once she'd begun.

"Em? Are you okay?" His eyes filled with concern. "It wasn't that funny. Actually, I didn't think it was funny at all. Just appropriate. "

She let the daggers fall to the floor, ignoring the clunking sounds as they hit the floorboards. "We made it." She threw her arms around him, kissing him as she held on tightly. Eventually she drew back slightly. "He's gone."

"I never doubted you'd manage. That we would manage."

"Really? Not even once?"

"Of course not. Essence is a demon and we're hunters. He didn't stand a chance. Especially not against you, someone born to be a hunter." He grinned.

"We are, are we?" She stressed the word 'we' each time she said it, wanting to make sure she'd understood what he'd said earlier.

He continued to hold her. "Yes, we are."

"Then it's probably time you started to train to become one. You can start with reading that book I gave you."

"Really? Wouldn't sword training be more practical?"

She pressed a finger against the hollow at the base of his neck. "You need a new cross. And no more calling on random fake gods."

"How was I supposed to know they existed?"

"I have a book you can read with a chapter about them." She wondered if it was still on the desk at Leo's house.

"When do we get to the sword training part?"

Before Emily could reply, a sound drew her attention to the front doorway. Leo stood there. She continued to stand where she was, holding onto Dante.

"Is he gone this time?" Leo asked.

Emily nodded.

"Then how about we go home? There are some people desperate to see Dante."

She held onto him for a few seconds more before slowly letting him go. He took hold of one of her hands before she could move completely away from him. She stared at him, a question in her eyes, but all she got from him in answer was a smile and a tightening of his hand on hers before he let go and helped to gather her weapons and ammunition before putting his shirt on.

It was a silent trip back to Leo's house and Emily drifted off to sleep where she sat in the front passenger seat. The moment they parked Jane ran towards them, pulling open the back door. Cricket jumped out, causing Jane to step back and let him pass.

"Mum is crying again." Jane sounded disgusted, her eyes red.

Getting out of the vehicle, Dante hugged his sister. "And you haven't been?" He let go of her.

Jane shrugged.

Emily started to walk towards the house when she saw the rest of his family come out the front door. Dante snagged her hand, drawing her back to him. She tilted her head to the side, about to ask what he wanted when he smiled, tugging her close enough to let go of her hand and slip his arm around her waist. She leaned against him, noticing Jane's speculative look.

When Rainbow reached them, she threw her arms around both Dante and Emily. "You're safe. It's all over?" Her gaze remained on Dante when she let go, her hands clasping one of his.

Dante glanced towards Emily before he met his mother's gaze again. "No, it's only beginning."

His comment brought a torrent of words. Arguments from Rainbow, pleas to be a demon hunter from Jane and questions on what it involved from Heathcliff. Emily was tempted to retreat to the house. Demons were easier to deal with. The only thing keeping her beside him was the way he held onto her so tightly. Not because she couldn't move away from him, but because he obviously needed her there.

Dante drew his hand from his mother's grasp. "How would you have felt if the hunters hadn't been there to help me? If they'd let me become a demon sacrifice?"

"You're safe now," Rainbow said.

"Yes. But how many others aren't? How many other mothers are wondering if their child is alive or will be found?"

"There are others who can do this. An entire family of them." Rainbow gestured towards Emily.

"But I know now." He stepped away from Emily, letting her go to take both of Rainbow's hands. "You taught us never to walk away from injustice. That pretending it doesn't exist is as bad as committing it yourself."

Rainbow stared up at him, tears pooling in her eyes. "I'm so proud of you." She pressed a kiss against his cheek. The one that had no blood on it. "Terrified, but proud."

Dante grinned. "Apparently it's sensible to be scared." He glanced towards Emily.

She returned his grin with a half smile of her own, taking the hand he held out to her. "You'll need training." She eyed him up and down. "A lot."

"And me? What about me?" Jane demanded.

"No," Rainbow said.

"But that's not fair. Same as Dan said. About injustice and all that," Jane said.

"No. Not another word on the subject, Jane." Rainbow glanced around the group. "How about some breakfast?"

Emily spoke when it looked like Jane would continue the argument. "Sounds good."

With a nod Rainbow headed for the house, Jane at her side arguing and Heathcliff trailing behind them. Dante walked at a slower pace, continuing to hold Emily's hand.

"I thought Heathcliff would be the one more interested in becoming a hunter than Jane."

"He is." Dante grinned. "He's waiting for Jane to wear Mum down before he starts."

"Smart thinking."

"Yeah, he'd make a good hunter."

She stopped walking so she could look at him. "He was born to be a hunter too?"

Dante laughed. "Yeah. Must run in the family." He tugged her against him, his lips briefly meeting hers. "Time for breakfast. Then sleep. After that, I think I need to start training. I've got a lot of years to catch up on." He slid his arm around her waist. "And we aren't starting with the book."

She couldn't stop a grin from escaping when she looked up at him, remaining at his side as they headed to the kitchen. The books were important too. He'd soon figure that out.

Chapter Twenty-Six

Emily held a white rose, staring at her parents' graves. A glance over her shoulder showed that Dante continued to wait for her. Even though her parents had lived in Mackay most of their lives, they were buried in a Brisbane cemetery. One filled with other Hunters. Even Patrick Hunter was buried here. She pushed thoughts of other Hunters away, focusing on why she'd come.

Laying the rose between their graves, she smiled. "I miss you. Both of you." She let the soft words hang in the otherwise silent air. "Every day." But she wasn't letting it stop her from living her own life. "I started uni, like we'd planned." Dante had too. They were doing different degrees, but were at the same university. She wished her parents could have met him.

"I miss being able to share things with you."

They'd talked about anything and everything. "I'm like Gran. I have premonitions. Only in my dreams though." She'd talked to Gran about them. It was the only time they came. She guessed it wouldn't be a good idea to go without sleep. "I no longer have nightmares." Now when she dreamt about her parents she got to revisit some of her favourite memories. The only time she saw them opening the door in her dreams was when she was about to have a premonition, but thankfully the premonition always arrived before the door was opened.

She'd also talked to Gran about why she'd dreamt of Dante so long after the first dream. She'd been partly right. It took two events to have premonitions for life. The death of someone you loved and someone, who had the potential to be your life mate, being in mortal danger. You couldn't get more dangerous than demons.

"They've locked up the ones who ordered your deaths. They're in a prison for the criminally insane." A smile momentarily appeared. "It was all over the news. You should have seen her yelling at the reporters, telling them they had no idea. Swearing that somehow she'd call Essence back to her and he'd get her out. She believes he's ignoring her because he's annoyed with her. He would go to her if he could. Not for her sake, but to escape. He's definitely stuck in hell." She hoped it was for a very long time. An eternity.

She glanced towards Dante and he smiled at her. After returning his smile, she faced the graves again. "I've learned I'm not a very good teacher." She had no idea how her parents had been able to teach her when she was so little. She hadn't realised how hard it must've been. "But he's learning. He also insists on joining me when I hunt." Gran had suggested she take on another partner until he was properly trained. She'd compromised. She went after the minor ones with Dante's help. If there were major demons, she called on her family.

"I returned home for a few days. Grandma and Grandad were relieved to see me. I could see they were sad when I told them I was remaining in Brisbane for now." Dante had gone with her. It had been strange returning home. There'd been so many memories. Everywhere she'd looked something had reminded her of her parents. One day that would be a good thing, but not yet. The distance would help. "They kept telling me how wonderful it was I was going to uni." It had felt like they were trying to convince themselves. They probably had been. She was going to miss them, but at least they were only a phone call away.

"I miss you so much." She took a step back from their graves. At least it no longer pained her almost physically to think about them. "I used to think I should have been there with you." Now she was mostly glad she hadn't been and that made her feel guilty sometimes. "I finished your last task for you. They saved six teenagers when they searched Susan's properties, after arresting her. Ones she'd planned to sacrifice for her beauty cream. It was all recalled and destroyed." They'd run tests and had come to the conclusion that none of the ones who'd been sacrificed had gone into the making of the cream. The news reports had talked about Susan's desperation to retain her youth, her mental decline and her belief in demonic cults to keep from ageing. They'd also said the beauty cream had been a hoax and it had been good genes keeping her and her grandfather looking younger than their years. Like their competitors had originally said.

Most people believed the news reports and many mocked her for believing in demons. A few realised the truth. Those were the ones who knew what Susan and Donald's incarceration really meant for the safety of humanity. She'd been tempted to send Susan a letter. 'Hunters are to be feared.' But the impulse had gone nearly the moment it had come. Susan would know she'd been wrong. Hunters were worth worrying about. She was living with the proof.

Donald wasn't faring any better than Susan. Where Susan had yelled and screamed and abused, he'd fallen silent and spoken to none. "Thank you for everything you taught me." She'd been born to be a hunter and they'd made certain she had the skills to be one. "I love you both." She blinked rapidly as she turned away, wiping at the corners of her eyes.

Dante walked towards her, taking her hand in his. "You ready to go?"

She looked towards the sky, very little light left. "Yeah, we better not be late." Her uncles had rung her twice already today. Both of them. Twice each.

Dante chuckled. "I think they're half expecting you to cancel on them again."

"That wasn't my fault. Demons are unpredictable." She walked beside him, heading for the exit of the cemetery.

"Maybe, but that doesn't change the fact they're probably worried you're going to cancel again."

"No, no cancellations." She glanced towards him, a smile slowly forming. "Although I did have a dream last night."

"Where did the dream take us?"

Us. She loved the way that word sounded. "I heard a clock strike midnight and I saw a street sign."

His hand tightened on hers. "Sounds like it might be fun."

"I'm not so sure about fun, but I can promise you won't be bored."

"If I've learned anything over the past couple of weeks, that's pretty much a guarantee. That and danger."

She came to a stop, facing him. Reaching up, she framed his face with her hands. "Does that bother you?"

"I trust you, Em." He grinned. "That and I'm sure I'm more than a little bit crazy since all this makes perfect sense these days."

A smile barely managed to form before his lips met hers and she wrapped her arms around him. Yeah, he probably was more than a little bit crazy. But then again, so was she.

Free Ebook

Sign up to Avril's newsletter to receive a free ebook. This ebook is exclusive to those on her mailing list. To find out more about this offer visit: http://www.avrilsabine.com/free-ebook/

*

We value your privacy and will not sell, rent, exchange or loan your email address to third parties. Your information is confidential and you are under no obligation to remain on the mailing list and can unsubscribe at any time.

Acknowledgements

As always, many thanks to my team for all the work they did in helping me improve and polish this novel. I dread to think of the amount of errors and problems my stories would have without all of you.

To The Reader

If you enjoyed this book, why not consider leaving a review to help other readers discover it too? Reader engagement is one of the few ways that lets an author know readers want more books in a particular series or genre. So leave a review and tell friends, not only about this book but also about other ones you've enjoyed, so you can continue to enjoy books by your favourite authors for years to come.

Dreams are meant to be lived,

Avril.

About The Author

Avril is an Australian author who lives with her family on acreage in South East Queensland. She writes mostly young adult speculative fiction, but has been known to dabble in other genres. You can find more information about her at her website www.avrilsabine.com where you can also subscribe to her newsletter to be kept informed about new releases, current projects, blog posts and exclusive news.

Titles By Avril Sabine

Stories about strong characters and characters who discover their strengths.

SERIES

Assassins Of The Dead- Young Adult Fantasy/ Paranormal

Book 1: Dark Blade

Book 2: Dragon Touched

Book 3: Society Against Vampires

Book 4: King's Request

Dragon Blood- Young Adult Urban Fantasy (with elements of romance)

(5 book series)

Book 1: Pliethin

Book 2: Wyvern

Book 3: Surety

Book 4: Knight

Book 5: Mage

Dragon Mage- Young Adult Urban Fantasy (with elements of romance)

(Series two of Dragon Blood series)

Book 1: Promise

Dragon Blood Chronicles- Young Adult Urban Fantasy (with elements of romance)

(Companion stand alone series to Dragon Blood)

Book 1: Oath

Book 2: Betrayed

Guardians Of The Round Table- Young Adult Fantasy LitRPG

(Co-written with Storm and Rhys Petersen)

Book 1: Dexterity Fail

Book 2: Goblin Boots

Book 3: Singed Feathers

Book 4: Frog Mage

Book 5: Crystal Mine

Book 6: Cursed Harp

Rosie's Rangers- Young Adult Western Steampunk

(6 book series)

Book 1: Justice

Book 2: Vengeance

Book 3: Treachery

Book 4: Accused

Book 5: Wanted

Book 6: Corruption

Mark Of Kings- Children's Fantasy

(Upper middle grade/preteen)

(4 book series)

Book 1: The Arena

Book 2: The Island

Book 3: The Assassin

Book 4: The King

STAND ALONE SERIES

Demon Hunters- Young Adult Urban Fantasy/ Horror (with elements of romance)

Book 1: Blood Sacrifice

Book 2: Retribution

Book 3: Tainted

Book 4: Premonition

Book 5: Cursed

Book 6: Feud

Book 7: Extrication

Plea Of The Damned- Young Adult Urban Fantasy/Paranormal

(6 book series)

Book 1: Forgive Me Lucy

Book 2: Forgive Me Aiden

Book 3: Forgive Me Jena

Book 4: Forgive Me Kobe

Book 5: Forgive Me Marti

Book 6: Forgive Me Dawson

Realms Of The Fae- Young Adult Urban Fantasy (with elements of romance)

The Sword (short story in Like A Girl Anthology)

Heart Of Stone

Book 1: A Debt Owed

Book 2: Marked By The Hunt

Book 3: The Magic Collector

Book 4: An Unexpected Betrayal

Book 5: Imprisoned By Iron

Fairytales Retold (Short Stories)

Snow-White And Rose-Red

The Twelve Brothers

The Light Princess

Beauty And The Beast

Sleeping Beauty

Aschenputtel

The Golden Bird

The Frog Prince

The Death Of Koshchei The Deathless

Myths And Legends Retold (Short Stories)

Ion, Son Of Apollo

Sir Gawain And The Maid With The Narrow Sleeves

Princess Ilse, The Giant's Daughter

YOUNG ADULT NOVELS

Young Adult Fantasy (with elements of romance)

Elf Sight

Earth Bound

Young Adult Urban Fantasy

Stone Warrior (with elements of romance)

The Jungle Inside

Young Adult Contemporary (with elements of romance)

Through Your Eyes

The Ugly Stepsister

Perfect Little Princess

Young Adult Contemporary/Paranormal

Whispers In The Dark (with elements of romance and same sex relationships)

Over Too Soon (with elements of romance)

Young Adult Sci-Fi

Experiment X-One-Six (Urban Sci-Fi/Superheroes)

An Endless Dawn (Post Apocalyptic Sci-Fi)

CHILDREN'S BOOKS

Dragon Lord (Preteen/early teens) (Fantasy)

The Irish Wizard (Upper middle grade) (Urban Fantasy)

SHORT STORIES

Urban Fantasy

Eternally Late

Dealings With Joe

Glimpses (short story in That Moment When Anthology)

Contemporary

The Brat Next Door

Fantasy LitRPG

(Set in the same world as Guardians Of The Round Table Series)

Tales Of Inadon 1: The Disc (Co-written with Storm and Rhys Petersen) (short story in Game On! Anthology)

Post Apocalyptic Sci-Fi

Compulsive Directive

NONFICTION

A Year Of Weekly Writing Exercises (Creative Writing)

Cooking For Families With Allergies (Cooking) (Co-written with Storm Petersen)

Tell Me A Story, Grandma (Memoir)

For the most up to date details on available titles visit:

www.avrilsabine.com/books/bibliography

Demon Hunters Series

To learn more about this series visit:

www.avrilsabine.com/series/dh

BOOKS AVAILABLE IN THE DEMON HUNTER SERIES

Book 1: Blood Sacrifice

Book 2: Retribution

Book 3: Tainted

Book 4: Premonition

Book 5: Cursed

Book 6: Feud

Book 7: Extrication

Disclaimer

This is a work of fiction. Names, characters, businesses, places, events and incidents are either the products of the author's imagination or used in a fictitious manner. Any resemblance to actual persons, living or dead, or actual events is purely coincidental. The opinions expressed or beliefs held are those of the characters and should not be assumed to be the opinions or beliefs of the author.

9 781925 131642